CHASE BRANCH LIBRARY
17731 W. SEVEN MILE RD.
DETROIT, MI 48235

MAY -- 2016

CH

CARTEL PUBLICATIONS
PRESENTS
Cherish's father warned her to watch the company she keeps. Now it's too late.
SKEEZERS
A NOVEL
By SHAY HUNTER

ARE YOU ON OUR EMAIL LIST?

SIGN UP ON OUR WEBSITE

www.thecartelpublications.com

OR TEXT THE WORD:

CARTELBOOKS TO 22828

FOR PRIZES, CONTESTS, ETC.

Check out other titles by The Cartel Publications

Shyt List 1: Be Careful Who You Cross
Shyt List 2: Loose Cannon
Shyt List 3: And A Child Shall Leave Them
SHYT LIST 4: Children Of The Wronged
Shyt List 5: Smokin' Crazies The Finale'
Pitbulls in a Skirt 1
Pitbulls in a Skirt 2
Pitbulls In A Skirt 3: The Rise Of Lil C
Pitbulls In A Skirt 4: Killer Klan
Poison 1
Poison 2
Victoria's Secret
Hell Razor Honeys 1
Hell Razor honeys 2
Black and Ugly
Black and Ugly As Ever
A Hustler's Son 2
The Face That Launched A Thousand Bullets
Year of the Crackmom
The Unusual Suspects
Miss Wayne and the Queens of DC
Paid In Blood
Raunchy
Raunchy 2: Mad's Love
Raunchy 3: Jayden's Passion
Mad Maxxx: Children of The Catacombs (Extra Raunchy)
Jealous Hearted
Quita's DayScare Center
Quita's DayScare Center 2
Dead Heads
Drunk & Hot Girls
Pretty Kings
Pretty Kings 2: Scarlett's Fever
Pretty Kings 3: Denim's Blues
Hersband Material
Upscale Kittens
Wake & Bake Boys
Young & Dumb
Young & Dumb: Vyce's Getback
Tranny 911
Tranny 911: Dixie's Rise
First Comes Love, Then Comes Murder
Luxury Tax
The Lying King
Crazy Kind of Love
Silence of The Nine
Silence of The Nine II: Let There Be Blood
Prison Throne
Goon
Hoetic Justice: eBook (Short Story)
And They Call Me God

WWW.THECARTELPUBLICATIONS.COM

SKEEZERS

By

Shay Hunter

Copyright © 2015 by The Cartel Publications. All rights reserved.
No part of this book may be reproduced in any form without permission
from the author, except by reviewer who may quote passages
to be printed in a newspaper or magazine.

PUBLISHER'S NOTE:
This book is a work of fiction. Names, characters, businesses,
Organizations, places, events and incidents are the product of the
Author's imagination or are used fictionally. Any resemblance of
Actual persons, living or dead, events, or locales are entirely coincidental.

Library of Congress Control Number: 2015958991

ISBN 10: 0989790126

ISBN 13: 978-0989790123

Cover Design: Davida Baldwin www.oddballdsgn.com
www.thecartelpublications.com
First Edition
Printed in the United States of America

What's Up Fam,

I hope this holiday season finds you in the best of health and full of love. I'm in awe that we are already in December. This year caught wheels on me and flashed by. Well, I am happy I was able to squeeze in a couple of quick getaways to regroup and refocus. No matter what your life may be requiring of you, it is imperative that you take self inventory and do something(s) for you.

On to the book in hand, "Skeezers"! I thought this was a great story. I don't want to say too much without spoiling it but just know I loved it and I'm sure you will enjoy it too.

With that being said, keeping in line with tradition, we want to give respect to a vet or a trailblazer paving the way. In this novel, we would like to recognize:

Ryan Coogler

Ryan Coogler is the young and talented writer and Director of, *"Fruitvale Station"* and brand new release, *"Creed"*. I loved his first film, *Fruitvale* but was in awe by the story he depicted in *Creed*. He not only wrote and directed a powerful, thrilling film, but he stayed true to the character and feel of the *"Rocky"* franchise. Whether you are a *"Rocky"* fan or not the story within Creed will leave you impressed and wanting more. I am a true *"Rocky"* fanatic and I absolutely loved the new age tale Coogler depicted. Not to mention that Sylvester Stallone and Micheal B. Jordan were phenomenal! Oscar worthy performances!

If you haven't seen it go to the THEATRE and check it out! No Bootleg, that's just gross.

Aight, get to it. I'll catch you in the next novel.

Be Easy!

Charisse "C. Wash" Washington

Vice President

The Cartel Publications

www.thecartelpublications.com

www.facebook.com/publishercwash

Instagram: publishercwash

www.twitter.com/cartelbooks

www.facebook.com/cartelpublications

Follow us on Instagram: Cartelpublications

#CartelPublications

#UrbanFiction

#PrayForCeCe

#RyanCoogler

#Creed

#Skeezers

CHAPTER ONE
SPYRELLA COMBS

I'm fat and ugly and I'm use to it now.

That's not my only problem. My pussy stinks when I walk. I can't move without sweating. My thighs rub together so much they are raw in the middle. When I move my arms jiggle and I have to sit down every so often to take a breath. It's so bad that I look away from mirrors for fear of hating myself so much that I finally decided to take my own life.

There's one reason I exist. Unlike some people who have great lives filled with loving friends, I enjoy my life in my dreams. In them I'm always who I want to be. In them I'm not a twenty-two year old horny person who can barely reach her own pussy to satisfy herself.

When I'm sleep all is well.

In my bed, my body drenched with sweat, I just awakened from another dream. In it my arms were raised over my head, my body moved like a ballerina as my partner lifted me off my feet and tossed me in the air before I landed in his arms. It was so real, when

I opened my eyes my calves throbbed. And that's when reality hit and I was reminded of my wretched life.

When my alarm went off I took two deep breaths and rolled onto my side. The irritating sound of the beeping caused me panic and I slammed my hand on top of the clock silencing it instantly. I must've been too hard because the screen cracked making it difficult to read the time.

Who needs a clock when everyday you do the same thing?

After five minutes I sat up on the edge of the bed, where it took me an additional five minutes before finally pulling my 330-pound frame off of my mattress. Out of breath already, I grabbed my burgundy robe and moved toward the dresser to get my watch that was almost too tight to fit on my arm.

If there was some way to get out of this body, to be the person I once was I would jump at it but I know that's impossible.

When I walked toward my bedroom door and pulled it open I sighed. Things were worse than I thought.

The living room floor was littered with beer cans, wine bottles and other trash. The light green couch had stains I didn't recognize and I saw crumbs everywhere. And when I glanced in the kitchen I saw a dish caked with the dried lasagna I made the night before for my cousins' party.

This is gonna take me all day.

After four hours I was almost done cleaning the living room when one of the three bedroom doors in the apartment opened. My cousin Carlita walked out, her fists pushing into her eyes as she yawned. I could smell the liquor all over her.

Her eyes were still red and her neck was covered in red splotches. Like me, my cousin is a redbone so whenever she's embarrassed, mad or experiencing a hangover it showed all over her face. "Damn, girl." She looked around. "We really did too much this time didn't we?" Her long light brown braids where rolled into a bun that sat on the top of her head.

I picked up a wine bottle and tossed it in the bag. "I'm fine. Most of it's done so it's not a big deal." It was more than a big deal. This shit was annoying but I could never say it. I could never say anything I felt because I knew no one would care.

"I'm not paying you no mind. I'm up and we not due at the club until later." She walked into the living room and helped. "You can't do this forever you know?" She dropped to her knees and picked up crumbs, tossing them into the trash bag. "You can't be this for the rest of your life, Spy."

"Let's not talk about that right now," I whispered. "Besides, she needs me."

"She'll be fine. Plus you the only one who doesn't have anybody in your life. She has Poe, whether he knows it or not and I got Wisdom. At some point she got to—"

Monique's door, closest to the front of the apartment opened and my naked cousin slid out holding a pill bottle. She was on so much medicine I couldn't keep up. She's tall, curvy, body the color of melted caramel and every time I see her it makes me sick with jealousy. I didn't always feel this way. When I was seventeen I use to look better than her, before my mother burned our house to the ground with me still in the bed. To save my own life I jumped out of a three-story window and broke my back in five places. For two years food and medicine was the only thing I could have and before I knew it I got like this.

Big.

And even though I understand on a regular basis that my weight is my doing I beg God every day to take the envy I have for her away.

It hasn't happened.

And I think she moved around the apartment naked on purpose, to torture me.

"What's taking you so long to clean up this fucking house, Spy?" Monique said as she opened the refrigerator and grabbed the milk carton. She pushed dirty paper plates that were on the counter onto the floor and sat on top of it. Bare assed. "And where is my breakfast? You know I have to eat to take my medicine."

"I can warm up a breakfast burrito."

"Well hurry up!"

I rushed to the freezer, removed the burrito and put it in the oven.

"Poe gonna be here in a minute," she continued. "And I do not want him to see this house like this."

From where she sat she opened the counter to the right, pulled out the coffee pot, all while drinking milk, lip to spout. I was always doing things for her hoping she'd appreciate me but she never did.

"Sorry, Mo. I just got up but I'm getting the place together now." I exhaled and wiped the sweat off my brow with the back of my hand. "It's just that there was so much stuff everywhere. It's taking me more time."

"Am I supposed to care?" she rolled her eyes and slammed the milk on the counter to her right. It splashed on her upper thigh. "The real problem is you're too fucking fat and you sleep all day." She paused. "But guess what, I don't pay you to sleep. The agreement was you cook and clean. If I got to see a mess, even one I made, it means I don't need you." She slid off the counter.

"You're right, Mo. I'm sorry."

"Sorry ain't enough. Me and Carlita the ones out here making money. So if you can't step up, step the fuck out."

I walked over to the sink and placed water in the coffee pot, added the grounds and put it on the stove to brew. So much sweat was pouring down my face now it started to burn my eyes. "After I make your coffee I'll get back to it."

From the corner of my eyes I looked at her body again. She and Carlita stripped in Washington DC but

Monique's body was so cold it was made for dancing. Before club Skeezers was vandalized and robbed, she was the headliner, pulling in drug dealers, ball players and wanna-bees from around the country. She made so much money that she had to be careful walking across the stage when she danced because it was littered with so many bills she would sometimes slip.

Although my original dream was to be an Alvin Ailey dancer I also thought endlessly about being a stripper at Skeezers. Poe, the owner, appreciated the art of dancing not just sexually. Whenever he came over he would give my cousins ideas on how to seduce with the eyes and it was Monique who took the advice to heart.

I can't count the number of times I tried to lose weight but in the end it was obvious that I would never win and dancing was not in my future.

Monique didn't have it all. She had the paper but she didn't have Poe. Who she really wanted. I never understood why he didn't see her that way. In my eyes she was perfect and so was he. At 6'2, with honey brown skin and a dick print I always seemed to notice, I often flipped my clit thinking about him.

But what could he do with a big girl like me?

I handed Mo her coffee and burrito, she snatched the food and stomped toward her room. Five seconds later she yelled, "Carlita, come back here with me! Let Spy do that shit herself. Poe on his way to pick us up to see the renovations and I don't want to be looking crazy when he get here."

Carlita handed me the bag of trash and gave me the sad look I hated. The one that said I was so pathetic that all she could do was feel sorry for me. "Let me go do her makeup. I'll see you in a minute. I'm sorry, Spy."

"It's cool." I smiled.

I cleaned the entire apartment in less than an hour and when I was done I was hungry. The moment my thoughts fell on my life I needed to eat whatever I could find. And since I was always depressed my appetite never stopped.

Feeling down I grabbed a half of strawberry cake from the fridge and the rest of the sour cream chips. With my hands stuffed I sat on the sofa and stuffed myself. Within seconds the chips were done and I was working on the cake when there was a knock at the door.

With my mouth full, my right hand still holding cake, I walked to the door before Monique came out screaming. Although I knew he was on his way, when I pulled the door open and saw Poe I wanted to pass out.

Wearing designer blue jeans and a white polo shirt, his muscles did a great job of representing themselves. He's so fucking sexy. He smiled at me and pinched my right cheek forcing a ball of chips from my lips that I hadn't chewed completely.

I was mortified as the crumbs fell to my feet.

I swallowed everything in my mouth and looked down at the floor at the mess. "I'm sorry…I was…I…" I bent down and picked up the food and held it in my free hand. "Sorry, Poe. This is bad."

He smiled wider. "Why you apologizing, beautiful?"

He played too much; calling me things he knew wasn't true.

"Don't know why you always seem stressed. It's never that deep with me." He winked and looked into the apartment. "Where's Mo and Carlita?"

"I'm right here," Monique said coming from behind. She bumped me with her hips on the way out the door and I smelled her expensive perfume. She was wearing tight black jeans and a cute white top with extra cleavage exposed. Her white and black Louis Vuitton purse dangled in her hand. "Why the fuck you always blocking the door, fat bitch?" She asked me.

"Come on, Mo, why you gotta be that way?" Poe frowned.

She waved him off. "Fatty knows I'm playing." She looked at me. "Right, Fatty?"

I nodded even though I wanted to cry.

"See, she's fine. Now let's go." She tapped him on the shoulder and switched to his black 7 series BMW sitting on the curb in front of the house. "I can't wait to see the additions to Skeezers."

When she slid into the passenger side Poe looked at me like he was sorry for me too. I hated that shit. "See you later, Spy." He winked and pinched my cheek again.

I smiled, nodded and watched him walk away.

"You okay?"

When I turned around I saw Carlita standing behind me. "Yeah," I lied.

"Remember what I said earlier?"

I didn't remember.

"You can't be this thing forever, Spy," She whispered. "You have to leave this house and live your life."

"Bitch, hurry up!" Monique yelled from the car. She rolled Poe's window down and screamed over him. "We don't got all fucking day!"

Carlita's body stiffened upon hearing her voice. Mo had a way of stuffing fear inside of the people who loved her the most.

Carlita hustled outside and slid into the car. Once she was inside I slammed the door, sat on the sofa and ate the rest of the cake.

It's settled.

I'm gonna take my life.

CHAPTER TWO

MONIQUE REDFIELD

"You wrong," Poe said as I looked for the Chapstick in my purse. "If you wanna carry shit like that with that girl don't do it near me." He continued to steer the car down the street. "I don't like it and it's fucked up."

I looked over at him and laughed. "What you talking about now, boy? Because you have to be the most sensitive man I know."

"I'm talking about Spy. And how you treated her back there."

I sighed. "I didn't do anything except tell the truth." I looked back at my cousin who was staring out the window. "Right, Carlita?"

She looked at me and nodded her head. "Yeah...right." She gazed back out the window.

Although she agreed with me I could sense her attitude. I didn't know if she thought I was being hard on Spy like Poe said or if something else was on her mind. She was so moody that I could never tell. All week I got the impression that she wanted to say something even though she never said shit.

It didn't make much difference if Carlita agreed about Spy or not. I'm so use to people, including my cousins, being jealous of me that I let most shit roll off my back. Besides, when it came to club Skeezers I was the one who brought in the dollars while Carlita and the other bitches picked up my scraps.

"Doesn't matter if Carlita agrees or not. You been coming down on Spy hard lately and all I'm saying is you should ease up. She's not somebody off the streets, she's your cousin."

I laughed. "Poe, you don't have to tell me who she is. And you don't know nothing about what goes on in my house either. If I didn't care about her I wouldn't say nothing. I'm hard on her so she can get her stuff together and that's our business."

"Nobody's gonna let you pound on them forever, Mo," he said.

"And like I said, you don't know what you're talking about." I smeared the strawberry Chapstick on my lips. "Ever since she broke her back she's been letting her body go and it's time for the pity party to end. What she gonna do? Eat herself to death?"

"You know that's not Spy's full story," Carlita interjected. "She eats for a lot of other reasons too."

I turned around and looked at her. "What you talking about? Aunt Diana? If you are she chooses to be homeless. You and me both know everybody has tried to get her off the streets, including my mother. And what did she do? Shoot everybody down. Anyway Spy has a home." I placed my purse on the floor. "Ya'll can keep feeling sorry for Spy if you want but I'm not giving out no pity points for a bitch who eats more than me. But both of you are welcome to it."

Poe shook his head and smirked. I loved Poe, wanted to be with him in a relationship and everything but sometimes he did things to irritate me. He cared too much about people and in my opinion it made him appear soft.

"Now what's funny?" I asked.

"One day she's gonna prove you wrong. She's gonna lose all that weight and give you a run for your money."

I looked at him for twenty seconds with a straight face and busted out laughing. Spy having it over me would never be possible. The girl was over three hundred pounds. "When that bitch loses weight I'll turn white. That much I can promise."

As I walked through the doors of Skeezers I was shocked. Before the club was vandalized it was a dark hole and every other thing was broken. I hated coming here sometimes because when it rained water dripped down the walls in the corners, making things smell musty.

Don't mistake me, we made money but I always knew if Poe put dough back into the club that it could be the gold pot it was born to be. I did everything I could do to get him to see things my way. I even begged but at the time he wasn't willing to reinvest capital into Skeezers. I found out when he was over the house for dinner that he had another plan.

After he ate my food and got drunk he said he was thinking about relocating to LA to run a restaurant with his cousin Quarry. It didn't matter that if he left I wouldn't have another place to dance. Nobody but

Skeezers gave me the star treatment and I didn't want that to change.

Just thinking about him leaving makes me sick to this day. But it's not all about the money. For as long as I can remember I wanted two things. The first was to get paid; preferably at Skeezers and the second was Poe Christopher. I practically owned Skeezers but he always seemed so out of touch. No matter what I said or did, he didn't look at me that way and didn't mind telling me.

I was forever stuck in the friend zone.

Throughout the time I knew him I was forced to see other females coming in and out of his life while I remained on the sidelines knowing all the while that he should be with me.

When he broke up with Vanessa, the night before the club was vandalized, I decided to make my feelings known. In the past I flirted with him but he always brushed me off. I needed to go harder.

On this particular night I had Spy make a big dinner and invited him over. When he got there I wasted no time. "Poe, I want to say something and I need you to hear me out. We've been friends for a long time and I've been holding this on my chest."

He laughed. "Mo, we only twenty-five. Ain't been out of school longer than seven years. Why so serious?"

"Because this *is* serious! I love you and it broke my heart having to see you with other girls knowing they could never treat you like I could. All I'm asking for is a chance and I promise, you won't regret it."

He cleared his throat and looked surprised. "I love you, Mo, I do. But not in that way."

I felt like the dining room was spinning. "But why?"

"Because...because I'm not attracted to you in that way. I look at you like a sister and I'm not trying to ruin what we got for nothing. You see how I be doing these women out here. I break a lot of hearts and I'm not about to do you the same way." He picked up his fork and started eating and I wanted to stuff it down his throat until it punctured the inner walls of his skin.

I remember being so angry my temples throbbed. The only reason I started dancing at Skeezers was because he begged. I use to dance around high school with Spyrella before she gained weight but never thought about being serious until he inherited the spot from his father.

I put myself out there, flashing my boobs and showing my pussy night after night, just to get him the come up I thought he deserved. And he still didn't want me! Well he didn't get to reject me and I decided to show him who was in charge. He needed to be starved of my love.

He had some friends but I was the best friend he had. For two weeks after he rejected me, I ignored all things Poe. He tried everything to reach out, from sending best friend forever teddy bears too my house, to sending tiny boxes from Tiffany's. No matter what he did I never bit. I wanted him to see how it would feel not to have me in his life and things were going good until Skeezers was vandalized.

Now let me be clear. I had *everything* to do with the vandalization. He was upset by the club being ruined, although I don't know why since he wanted to leave it anyway, I really did it for the insurance money. I figured if I paid somebody to fuck it up enough he would have the right cash and we could start all over in a new place.

He was sad when he knocked on my door with the news, telling me how badly it was destroyed. He looked so pitiful that the bitch in me couldn't turn him away, besides I missed him and punished him enough. With the lines of communication reopened we talked about all possible scenarios for the new and improved Skeezers. At first he was acting like the club being ruined was another reason to go to LA but I think he really missed me. And since I didn't live there, he would have to stay here.

He shocked me and decided to have it repaired.

After spending every day together while the club was getting fixed, we stayed on the couch, watched Netflix and I felt at home with him. He made it clear that he needed me as much as I needed him, even if it were just as friends. But I didn't want friendship. I wanted a husband. I knew it would take a little longer to make him my husband and the plan was to now move slowly.

As I walked deeper into Skeezers I ran my hand over the liquid shiny marble stage. Next I eyed the wall fish tank that stood behind it and glanced at the pole that sparkled with gold flakes. The scent of the leather furniture was thick and everything about the club screamed new.

He walked up behind me and rested his hand on my shoulder. "What you think? Because I been waiting on your opinion for a minute."

I exhaled and shook my head softly. "Oh, Poe, it's fucking beautiful!" I looked at Carlita who already managed to crawl her ass on the stage. Showing off, she gripped the pole, pulled herself to the top and slid down headfirst.

I rolled my eyes.

Poe removed his hand off me and clapped at Carlita's fake ass show. Bitches stay vying for his attention, especially those with my blood in they're veins it seems. "I guess you ready to get back to spinning huh?"

Carlita stood up and said, "I can't lie, it's nice as hell." She looked around. "Females gonna trip over their faces trying to come up in here."

"I hear you, but is it nice enough for you to come back?" He asked. "When we were vandalized we lost five girls to other clubs. The only people left is Mo, Tudy and Brenda. I need you."

She shrugged. "Don't know about that, Poe. You know I have to talk to Wisdom. He never was feeling me working here."

"But he met you here." I said.

"Well he sees more for me in life then showing my ass." She looked at Poe. "No offense."

He raised his hand. "None taken. I don't want either of you here longer than you have to be. So I understand Wisdom. Respect."

I rolled my eyes. Not only because she had to talk to Wisdom about everything *before* she did it but also because she acted like he was her father. She could fake in front of Poe if she wanted but she was gonna strip in this bitch just like I was. How else would she earn money?

"Well he'll be here in a minute," Poe said glancing at his silver Rolex. "Ask him then." He returned his hand to my shoulder and electric currents exploded through my body. "Ready to see your dressing room?"

I turned around and looked up at him. "*My* dressing room?" I pointed to myself.

"Yeah…you bring in the ballers, Mo and I'm not telling you anything you don't already know. You deserve your own space so I made it happen." He took me by the hand and pulled me away.

As we moved down the hall and toward a burgundy door I saw a gold star on it. Under the star was my name written in black. This door was never here before so I figured like he said he had it built for me. When I glanced down the other end of the hall I saw the old dressing room, which looked like it was also revamped.

"Poe..." I covered my mouth. "This me for real?"

"Open the door and see."

I twisted the knob and was dumbfounded by what I saw. If he didn't prove to me how much he wanted me before I knew now. My personal space was perfect. It was built for a superstar! Directly in front of me was a huge mirror surrounded by lights that sat on a vanity. The color scheme was pink and gold. I could eyeball the furniture and tell not one item was cheap. He really went all out with the insurance money he got from the vandalizing. He had to add some money to this. "Poe, how much was all of this?"

"Not merely enough." He winked.

"Seriously. When we talked about the insurance policy you told me how much you were getting." I looked around. "This room alone looks like it took half of that amount."

"Let me worry about that," he said looking into my eyes. "You should've been treated like this before, Mo.

If you ask me I'm late showing you." When his phone rang he removed it from his pocket and looked down at it. It was probably one of his groupie bitches. Poe had about five or six females who were in different slot positions to be his girl. My plan was to bump them all down and take first place, but I had to play it smooth. Which was hard for a bitch like me, use to getting her way.

"Wisdom at the bar. Gotta show him how the register works and then I'll be back." He kissed me on the cheek and walked out just as my mother was walking inside.

Poe hugged her before leaving.

She looked around him, her jaw hung as she moved inside of my dressing room. Tossing her black purse on my pink chaise. "Bitch, you not gonna tell me that nigga don't love you!"

"Levine!" I yelled. "He gonna hear you."

"I don't give a fuck if he do. I'll only be telling the man what he knows already." She placed her hand on her hips, which were wrapped in tight jeans. She was 45 but looked 30 easily. I don't know if it was her trendy clothing or her up to date hairstyles but she always looked nice. "Don't get mad at me because I was right!" She walked around my dressing room and touched everything in sight. "Finally a nigga who knows how to treat my daughter and it's about time."

"You're over-reacting, Levine."

"No!" she stuck her long red nail in my face. "What you need to be doing is having a baby by his fine ass. I been working at this club since his daddy owned it and the only thing I got when he died was 5% ownership."

"But you made a lot of money when you sold it to Poe so don't act like that."

"I would've made more had I held out for the vandalism check. And anyway I'm not talking 'bout the money. Women ain't supposed to be flashing pussy past 30, Mo. You supposed to get yourself a husband and settle down because I don't want you in here like me." She moved closer. "Now I don't care what you got to do but that's your nigga out there!" she pointed at the door. "And you better not let another bitch snatch him up. If you do it'll be your fault and you'll never be able to forgive yourself."

CHAPTER THREE

CARLITA FIELDS

I walked past Monique's dressing room on the way to the bathroom. When I glanced inside she was standing in front of her vanity and I was amazed how a soft glow always seemed to surround her. I know it's a bit much but in my opinion there's not a more beautiful woman in the world and that includes me. She has it over everybody in the looks department. She would be next to perfect except for one thing.

She was mean as fuck.

After going to the bathroom I walked to the bar. My boyfriend Wisdom was standing behind it, his eyes glued on the fancy new cash register screen that glowed on his face. People always looked at us funny whenever we went anywhere due to our height. He's 6'4, which meant he towered over my 4'11 inch frame.

When I met him here three years ago he said one thing. "You gonna be my bitch and when you do you gonna come off that pole."

I never met another man more diligent than he was. Everyday he would post up in front of the stage as I danced. When people tipped me he was fine but if they tried to touch me he'd let them know I was his wife. It didn't bother me that he was lying or that he was coming on strong. The only person mad about it was Mo because I think she wanted him too and he was never interested. In the end she left us alone and told me I would soon find out about the man he was and so far all I saw were good things.

Well, sometimes…

"You seem out of it," I said walking up behind him, resting my head on the middle of his back. "Everything okay?"

He pushed a few buttons and my body moved every time he did. He seemed frustrated as he stabbed the keyboard. "I don't know what's wrong with this bitch! Poe should've kept the old one. He knows how I feel about new shit."

I frowned. "I thought Poe showed you how to use it." I walked to the side of him to get a better view and to see if I could help.

"He spent a quick five on me but the nigga so pressed to get ready for opening night tomorrow that he rushed me through it. You know I'm not up on computers and shit."

"Want me to help?"

He waved me off. "I got it."

He didn't like me to see he couldn't do something, even if I could help. So I walked around the bar and sat on a barstool. Without looking at me he walked to the new cooler, grabbed a Corona, popped it open and sat it in front of me before busying himself with the cash register again.

I took a gulp. "Thanks, bay." I raised the beer.

"Don't worry about it." He continued to work.

"You know he asked me again."

He stopped moving, his fingertips hovering over the register. "No." He went back to stabbing at it. "And it's settled so ain't no need in you pressing the issue."

"But we need the money, Wis. You do all you can for me and I want to help out too."

He sighed, walked around the bar and sat next to me. Holding my hands he looked into my eyes. "I've never asked you for a dime. Ever. Plus we have over forty thousand dollars saved. Forty."

"Wisdom..."

"Listen, I know when I met you, you were a dancer. And I know I told you I could handle it but I lied. What's mine is mine and it ain't nobody else's business."

"But you saw how hard it was for you to get at me. I'm not loose with my body, Wisdom. And I'm in a relationship so I would never talk to another man or disrespect—"

"Your body is sacred and it's mine and I don't want you showcasing it anymore. Am I clear? Because if we gonna go forward I have to know that right now."

I rolled my eyes. "Wisdom…"

He let my hands go. "Is that the kind of man you want?"

I raised my eyebrows. "Huh?"

"Why would you want a man who's okay with you parading your body around a strip club? Even with the renovations it's not worthy of you." He placed his hand on his chest, directly over his heart. "You did what you felt you needed to in the beginning and I fully respect that, but you're in a relationship now and your man is asking." He grabbed one of my hands. "Begging, that you give this thing up."

I knew he was right but the type of woman he wanted me to be I wasn't sure if I could handle. If he had it his way I would stay home, barefoot with a spatula while he brought home the money. I love Wisdom, more than anything, but I'm afraid of being totally dependent on anybody. That's partially the reason I didn't tell him about the fifty grand I had saved in a private account.

"Okay..."

"Okay what?" he asked.

"Okay I won't dance again."

He hugged me and kissed me deeply, reminding me in seconds that for me there was nobody else. "You won't be sorry, Carlita. I promise you." He stood up, walked behind the bar and fussed with the cash register again. "You told her already right? Because it's only a matter of time before we move."

I was ashamed. "No..."

"Bay, why not?" he paused. "We had a plan and now you're changing it."

"I haven't changed a thing, Wisdom. Just didn't tell her yet that's all."

"You were supposed to tell her last week. What you gonna do when it's time for us to move into our house? Move out at the last minute? Without giving her notice?"

"You don't understand. The three of us have taken care of each other so long that I don't think she'll be able to handle it."

He frowned and stuffed his hands into his jean pockets. "Then what are you saying? That you're not moving with me? That you're gonna spend the rest of your life with your cousins?" He laughed.

"Of course I'm not saying that."

"Then it's simple. We're moving into our home in three months and you're moving in with me in my apartment in a month. In order to do that you gotta tell her, Carlita. I let Monique come in the way of our relationship too long. I'm done with that and you should be to."

If only things were that easy. I knew immediately that all hell was about to break loose in my world.

I could feel it.

CHAPTER FOUR
SPYRELLA

I lit the third coconut-scented candle and walked into the kitchen to check on the steaks in the oven. I was preparing them with cheddar-mashed potatoes, biscuits and spinach. I had an apple pie on the side that I would cook once dinner was done because I wanted things nice. After hearing Monique's voice I realized things needed to be perfect.

When Monique called earlier and told me what she wanted to eat I was in a good mood because she sounded happy, excited about the club opening and for some reason I was too. Maybe it was because lately she spent too much time here while the club was being fixed. And since she was *always* home she *always* found more to complain about.

When I placed the finished meal on the warmers I turned up the radio, which was on the quiet storm. Chris Brown's song '2012' blasted from the speakers and standing in the kitchen I danced as the music moved through my soul. Other than when I was eating the only time I felt alive was when I was dancing. And I only did that when I was alone or in a good mood.

I kept my eyes closed and for the moment I wasn't some big woman who lost touch with her body. I was slim and in shape like I had been before my world came to an end.

I was dancing off the second verse when I heard Carlita giggling. "Looking good, cousin!" She was clapping excitedly and behind her stood Poe and Monique, who didn't seem too happy.

My body felt flushed.

"Damn, girl you still got moves," Poe said. "I see you over there." He nodded.

I turned the music at a low level and tried not to grin. "Don't play, Poe." I moved to the stove and stirred the mashed potatoes. "I was just goofing off. No need for charity compliments."

He walked deeper inside and stood behind me. I felt his eyes all over me and I didn't understand why. If he didn't stop staring I was gonna vomit because I imagined all of the things he was pointing out wrong with my body. "I don't say things I don't mean. You really looked good. You should get back to what you love."

"He's right, Spy. You still got that shit!" Carlita said moving closer. "Plus it's a good way to workout!"

I considered what they were saying when I looked into their eyes and saw the seriousness. Maybe I could dance again. Maybe if I tried hard enough I would lose the weight. I started to consider the impossible until I heard Monique's screeching laughter. "I was gonna stay quiet but now ya'll doing too much. Got this girl in here thinking big bitches are supposed to be dancing sexy."

"Monique, leave it alone," Poe snapped. "If you feel differently keep it to yourself. This is just me and Carlita's opinion."

"Which part of it do you want me to leave alone? The part that you lying to my cousin or the part that she so dumb she might be over there believing you?"

Everyone was standing in the kitchen, a place I considered my own. No one ever came in here unless they wanted me to cook and I didn't realize until that moment how much I liked it that way. Isolation has benefits. It prevents you from getting your feelings hurt.

"She's right," I said walking around them toward the refrigerator. I had tasted the mashed potatoes and they weren't cheesy enough so I needed to fix them. "I was just fooling around. I'm not even into dancing anymore. Gave it up a long time ago."

"You see, even she knows she's a fat mess," Monique said throwing her arms up before allowing them to drop to her sides. I didn't know she was so close to my body until she grabbed a handful of the flesh on my arm and wiggled it. "I mean look at this shit, she's massive." She released. "Before she even thinks about dancing anywhere let alone in public she needs to be working out in the gym.

"After all these years you still don't know what to say out your mouth," Poe said. "I'm going in the living room. Let me know when dinner's ready, Spy. By the way everything looks good. Thank you for cooking for me." He smiled at me and looked at Mo angrily.

From the corner of my eye I saw Carlita looking at me intensely. Like she felt sorry for me again.

Suddenly I was overwhelmed and I ran out of the kitchen and into my room, slamming the door behind myself. Lying face down on the bed I was mad when five minutes later the door opened. Without even looking I knew who it was. "Go away, Carlita. I want to be alone right now."

"I'm leaving..."

I turned my head to the side to look at her. "What you mean?"

"I'm moving out and you should go too. One of the reasons I stayed so long was because I was worried that you would never go if I left first."

"It's not that easy for me." I sat up in the bed and looked over at her. "If we go, if we leave, she'll—"

"Have to take care of herself." She shrugged. "Nobody wants to leave her less than me. I know she talks a lot of shit and is more bark than bite. Still the way she treats you is unacceptable, Spy. Go, and live your life."

"But where? I've never been anywhere but here."

"Anywhere is better than this. And don't say you don't have the money because you've been saving thousands of dollars. I wouldn't be surprised if you have over 100 thousand saved."

I laughed. "Only $45,000."

She chuckled. "You see, plenty." She shoved my arm.

"But I've never lived on my own. What will I do?"

"You will live your life."

"Should I tell her?"

Carlita sighed. "I think you owe her at least that but if you don't she deserves that too."

I hated to admit it but as mean as Mo was to me, I was afraid. Afraid of what it meant to be on my own and afraid of leaving Monique. But Carlita was right; it was time for me to move on.

CHAPTER FIVE

SPYRELLA

I sat in the car I never used unless I was grocery shopping and stared at my mother.

She was sitting outside, on a park bench, with three equally dingy men standing in front of her. She looked engaged in conversation but I didn't understand how it was possible to be happy with nothing. She didn't have a home. I never did fathom how she could live outside year after year no matter the conditions.

My mother gave up on life a long time ago, when she burned down our house after my father left her for a white woman. Dad cheated before but no other woman sent her through the roof but Beth. When asked why, after she was arrested and put in prison for five years she said, "I can be skinnier. I can get plastic surgery to be prettier. But if he wants a white woman I can't compete."

My dad and Beth were murdered after her boyfriend found out they were getting married but my mother still went deeper into depression. After getting released from prison she vowed never to build a home again, despite my needing her help.

When she was sent away it was my aunt Levine who treated me okay, just as long as I knew that Monique was her pride and joy. If she bought Monique new clothes for school she would make sure they were designer, while I got stuff from Target or Wal-Mart. I knew she cared about me but there was always a difference.

Growing up without my mother made me miserable.

I got out of my car and walked toward the bench. A dirty man who wore a stained, brown button down looked at me and said, "Diane, is that your daughter?"

My mother turned around and her expression flattened when she saw my face. She wasn't cheerful like she was moments earlier. Once again she was unhappy to see me. "Yeah, she's mine." She slid off the bench and walked toward me, her hands stuffed into her pockets.

Her hair was braided but you could tell they'd been in so long that they dreaded. I could smell the dried urine that soaked itself into her clothing and wanted to throw up as she moved closer. The scent was overpowering.

I was about to back up but she hugged me, her onion scented underarm near my nose. I held my breath and didn't breathe again until she released me. "What you doing here, Spy? I...I didn't expect you. I would've cleaned up a little."

I don't know how you gonna do that.

"I know, ma, just wanted to see you that's all so I popped up." I felt uncomfortable looking at her. Smelling her. "I'm just happy I didn't miss you. I've been here before but you weren't home...I mean...around."

She cleared her throat. "Is everything cool with you?" she looked me over, maybe checking for bumps or bruises. "You looked like you gained a little more weight, Spy." There was a nervous smile on her face. "You were always so thin and beautiful. Now...well now..."

I tried to hold back my tears. Besides, there was no use in crying. I had a plan and it was simple. And because she ruined my life I wanted her along for the ride when I finished. "I know, Ma. I guess life got in the way. Not everybody can have it all like you. In this perfect world."

Her light brown skin reddened. "I deserved that," she said.

I shrugged.

"You know I'm not trying to be mean, Spy, it's just that I haven't seen you in months."

"I guess I don't get out much. But I'm here now."

She frowned and looked confused. "Wait, is my sister okay?"

Since Carlita's mother joined a convent when Carlita was five, I figured she was talking about Aunt Levine. "Haven't seen her but I think she's okay."

She nodded. "So what did I do to deserve this visit?"

I wanted to ask her why she chose this life like I had so many times. But I also knew she was tired of the same questions. At the end of the day she was where she wanted to be. "If I got a place, something big enough for both of us, would you give it a try and live with me?"

She sighed and moved her head from left to right as if frustrated. You would've thought I asked to borrow money. Instead I was offering her the chance to have a warm place to sleep and shower.

At least for a little while.

"I don't know, Spy you know how I feel about sponging off folks."

"But I'm not folks, I'm your daughter."

"But how would I pay my own way? I don't even have a job."

"Well how do you take care of yourself out here, ma? One of them men looking out?"

She looked away from me and then at the ground. "We have people who come through to give us food and stuff. Some kind of way I always make it work."

"Well I want to do the same thing for you. I would take care of you until you got on your feet."

She rolled her eyes and tucked her hands under her pits. "Just like I thought, sponging."

I exhaled. "Ma, I don't like you out here. And I know you consider this place home but it's not. Don't make no sense you here when you have family who would be willing to let you stay if you asked."

"What family?" she asked sarcastically. "My sister Levine who spit on me when I accidently sat on her sofa? Even though I didn't want to go to her house but went only because she begged and said she missed me? Or are you talking about that mean ass niece of mine who is so evil you can see the 6's on her forehead?"

I shook my head. "As mean as Monique is she has asked you to stay with her plenty of times."

"She did that because people think I'm charity. The thing to do when your life is fucked up and you want to make the world a better place. But like I said, I'm good out here."

"You abandoned me as a child, ma. You left me alone just because a man didn't want you. He left, but I didn't and all I'm asking is that you stay with me for a few months *now*, while I get on my feet. Can you do one thing for me, finally? So that I don't have to be alone."

She looked like she was thinking about it. "I don't know about living with you, Spy. I would feel…I would feel…unwanted."

"Mama, I'm going through something. I guess more mental than anything but I need you. I need you with me."

She looked at me, looked up at the sky and back at her friends who were cracking open a can of beer. "I can't." She leaned in and kissed me on the cheek forcing me to smell her body odor again. "I'm sorry." She turned around and joined her friends.

I looked at the piece of paper in my lap and back at the single brick home. The address appeared correct so I figured this was the place. I took a deep breath and pushed out of my car. When I knocked on the door I was about to turn around when an elderly white lady with a grey beehive opened it. "Spyrella Combs?"

I turned around and smiled. "Uh, yes. It's me."

"Did you want to see the house?"

I swallowed. "It's still available?"

"Of course. And since I have to move down south to be with my sick mother I'm willing to knock off a few hundred dollars a month. Bringing the price to $1,100."

I thought about my life and my plan to get my mother back. Seemed like a nice enough place despite not going inside yet. "I'll take it."

She laughed. "But you haven't seen it yet."

"Trust me, I know I want it."

"Well come on inside to see your new home."

She didn't know but the conditions wouldn't matter anyway. My plan was to tie my mother downstairs, set the house on fire and then take my life.

I just wanted to make sure she watched me end it.

CHAPTER SIX

MONIQUE

Eyes still closed, I rolled over, reached out and touched the cool side of my bed. The place where Poe was before I went to sleep. I tried my best to stay up last night when we were up watching television, knowing that if I didn't when I woke up he'd be gone.

Last night, after eating, he followed me to my room fully clothed. He was still hot over the words I had for Spy but after awhile he got over it.

We talked about the past, when we were in school and all the crazy shit that happened to us. He thanked me for being by his side again while he reopened Skeezers and although my pussy was juicing and I wanted to fuck, he chose to lay next to me and stroke my hair probably knowing I'd fall to sleep.

Irritated, head throbbing, I stomped toward my door and pulled it open. I didn't smell food, which was fucked up because Spy knew she had to cook every morning, especially on the days I worked late at the club. I couldn't take my medicine without food.

She's a selfish bitch.

Because of all of the things going on in my life, mostly negative, I was on a lot of meds. I took something for depression, something for migraines and something for my neck. It was broken two years ago when I was raped after leaving Skeezers.

The rapist waited until I came outside, slammed his hand over my nose and mouth and dragged me in an alley. I was on the ground when he ripped my pants off and shoved his penis inside me while my neck was on two bricks that must've fell off the wall. I was in severe depression for six months and for real I haven't been right since.

For one I hated being alone, which is why I had two roommates. And secondly I get nervous if my world changes in any way. I liked things to stay the same because it's how I maintained my sanity. Most people liked new and exciting things but not me. That's why I didn't leave Skeezers even though I could go to more luxurious spots and get more money.

This is why I've been in this house since I bought it the first year I started stripping because it was mine and it was home. And this is why I didn't want Poe to leave me.

No changes!

Ever!

When I walked into Spy's room to wake her fat ass up I was surprised that everything was neat. Too neat. Normally she'd have clothing hanging off her mirror so she couldn't see her fat face, along with stuff thrown all on the floor. Now as I looked around I didn't see anything. When I walked to her closet I was shocked. Everything's gone.

When did she leave?

I rushed out of her bedroom and looked around the kitchen. It was clean but I could sense that she hadn't been here. Spy would never have done anything like this on her own.

"She moved out," Carlita said leaning on the frame in her own bedroom doorway. "Last night I think."

I walked up to her. "You mean you knew this shit and didn't tell me?"

"To be honest, Monique I didn't think you would care." She scratched her head and yawned. "Every time you talk to her you're screaming. I don't think she could take it anymore."

I opened my mouth but the words didn't come out. To be honest I don't know why I was finding this so hard to believe. "If Spy got mad because I didn't want her going out here in these streets flaunting her body around, knowing how people feel about fat people, then let her be mad."

"You hurt her on a daily basis, Mo. You know I love you but you can be harsh sometimes. Even Poe said that."

I laughed. "So now I'm the bad guy?"

"I don't think you're bad but Spy looks up to you and I think you really got to her last night."

"You know what, I don't even care. I mean think about all the things we do for her around here." I paused. "All she has to do is cook and clean and we pay her thousands a month. Didn't even charge her rent."

"We didn't charge her rent but she had to cook breakfast, lunch and dinner. On top of that she cleaned your room in the morning and mine on Sundays. She was a maid, Mo, and I guess she wasn't feeling it anymore. If you ask me she's entitled to live her life." She walked into the living room and plopped on the couch. "A girl gets tired after awhile I guess."

I sat next to her and brought my knees to my chest. "I hear all that but she could've been a woman and said it to my face. I could've gotten someone else to stay here with us. You know I need help around here." I looked into Carlita's eyes and saw she seemed out of it.

What did she want to say?

"I got to tell you something, Mo," she said under her breath. "You not gonna like it but I don't have a choice. I'm moving out too."

My eyes widened and my pulse quickened. I jumped up, rushed to the bathroom in my room and pulled open the medicine cabinet. I could feel a headache coming and figured it was my blood pressure. My mother said I was too young for these types of problems but not many girls had a life like mine either.

I tossed the pills in my mouth, turned on the sink and cupped handfuls of cool water, splashing it against my lips. When I was done Carlita was standing behind me. "You know what hurts me the most, that you knew she was leaving and you're doing this to me. We family, Carlita. Is this how you do family?"

"I'm not trying to hurt you, Mo. It's just that Wisdom has been nice about this arrangement. He understood that we lived together and after the rape told me to stay, even though I was supposed to move in with him that week. He wants me with him now and I don't blame him."

"You always crazy over niggas. You known him for some years but I've been your cousin all your life."

She walked inside and sat on the toilet lid while I leaned against the wall and stared at her. I didn't know what was going to have to happen but I could not live by myself.

"It's not like that, Mo. I love Wisdom and he wants a family. I want one too. Can't you understand that?"

She sounded stupid. Why was she tripping off a nigga who was clearly trying to control her? "Keep shit straight. When are you leaving?"

"A few months. Maybe one."

I felt my stomach swirling and I started hyperventilating. Carlita stood up and placed her hands on my shoulders but I left the bathroom, unable to breathe. "I can't...I can't...believe you leaving so soon! You not giving me a chance to do anything!"

"Monique, you'll be fine and I'll be by to— "

"But you won't be here," I cried. "If I have a nightmare when I'm alone..." She exhaled. "I'm not gonna lie, if you leave here now, knowing how I need you we're done. I don't want you to ever say anything else to me."

She sat on the sofa and tossed her face in her hands. "How much time do you need?"

I plopped next to her. "Six months...you give me that and I can find a new roommate. And I'll be nicer to you and everything!"

She leaned back and looked up at the ceiling. "Wisdom is going to kill me."

"If he loves you then he'll understand." I placed my hand over hers. "Please, Carlita. It's blood before everything and he gonna have to respect that. Right?"

CHAPTER SEVEN
CARLITA

He was laying on the bar, naked from the waist down, dick pointed in the air. I crawled on top of him and nestled my pussy over his stiffness. Since my feet didn't have anywhere to go, one hung off the bar stool to the left and the other rested in the sink behind the bar.

Wisdom moved in and out of me as he pressed into my wet pussy. He had been teasing me all night and although the club was opening up in less than two hours it was obvious he could no longer resist or wait for us to get to his apartment.

As we fucked harder I could feel him throbbing and pulsating and I felt bad. Not because we were having sex, which I loved, but because as hard as he was I realized it had been awhile since I gave him pussy.

Monique was such a handful that by the time he got off work and I got to his house, I was so tired I would fall into a coma like sleep. I guess I was depriving my man of sex and I'm surprised he was still here. I knew other dudes who would've left a long time ago.

Mine didn't.

When he applied more pressure on my hips and into my pussy, I thought I would split open. The stare he gave me was a cross between love and hate and it made me want him even more. Every time he banged into me my clit vibrated and I knew I was about to explode.

Right before I came he lifted me up and positioned me so that my titties and belly were pressed against the bar. Within seconds he eased into me again but this time he fucked me harder from the back. My chin stabbed into the cool marble as I moved up and down. I came so hard I screamed out into Skeezers and my temples throbbed. He must've gotten his too because I felt his warm sperm on my butt, before he wiped it off roughly with a couple of hard, dry paper towels.

He slapped my ass. "I needed that, Carlita. Good looking out."

I felt like a whore but he always made me feel that way when he was fucking to get something off his mind.

After we were dressed I helped him wipe down the bar and I could tell something was still wrong. Part of me didn't want to bring more bad news his way by telling him I couldn't move.

As I dunked my rag into the Pine Sol water in the bucket I said, "What's wrong, Wisdom? I figured you'd be happy with Skeezers opening back up tonight."

He exhaled. "I am, just some things on my mind that's all."

"Like what?"

"My father's locked up again." He wiped the counters down behind the bar and avoided eye contact with me. "I hope they keep the nigga this time because I'm tired of him breaking my grandmother's heart."

My eyebrows rose and I walked up to him. "Damn, Wisdom, I'm sorry. What he do?"

"They say he murdered Liz but they still building a case."

I felt gut punched. Liz and Wayne had been together for twenty years and I couldn't see him hurting her, let alone killing her. Whenever they were together he was so attentive, even though people said he had a violent side. The scariest part is that everyone said that Wayne and Wisdom looked and acted the same way.

"But it doesn't make any sense. They were gonna renew their vows and everything. Are the police sure? Sometimes they just want the case closed without finding out who's really responsible."

"Nobody's sure about shit in this world, Carlita." He turned toward me, leaned against the cabinet and crossed his arms. "But you know how he is. Everybody knows how he is. He can snap if pushed."

I ran my fingers through my braids. "I know you've told me he's been a little violent before but still he hasn't done anything like this. Right? It seems so out of character."

"Damn, I wish you would stop acting so fucking naive!" he yelled in my face. "If I ever got locked up for some shit I expect you to take it like a woman instead of running around asking why!"

I jumped back afraid he would lash out violently. Wisdom was right. I did know Wayne to have a temper because like everybody knew, Wisdom did too. He never hit me and hardly ever yelled but when he did I always felt like a child. Quiet. Meek. And unable to defend myself.

Monique said he picked me because he knew I could easily be manipulated. I remembered being so mad when she first said it that I didn't talk to her for two days. But now, well now I'm not so sure. Most girls would've probably cursed him out or slapped him for how he just jumped. But whenever he yelled at me I took it as another reason to leave him alone and so I gave him his space. My only focus was keeping him in my life and not losing him. "I know you're upset but I have to talk to you about something."

"I'm sorry," he exhaled walking up to me. It was like a switch was clicked back on and now he was a different person. "I didn't mean to come at you like I did just now. It's just that me and pops always have been close and I didn't expect it to bring me down." He pulled me closer and kissed me deeply. I could smell the sweetness of my pussy all over him. "That's why I want to be with you, so I'm not alone when I got shit I'm going through." He exhaled. "I just want to get you in our home and I promise I'll be a better man."

"That's what I want to talk to you about." He released me. "I can't go." I don't know why I blurted it out. I guess I knew if I didn't tell him now I never would.

"What do you mean you can't go?" He scanned me from my toes to my eyes. "Make it clear."

I stepped back. "I mean I can go, just not now."

"You mean to our…our home?"

I nodded yes.

He backed away and leaned on the counter again. "Fuck, Carlita! How much longer you gonna let your cousin ruin what we have? I mean do you think if she had a nigga she would let you do it to her?"

"It's not what it sounds like, Wisdom. Spy left last night, I mean she moved out and now Monique is by herself."

"Good! She had the guts to roll out and I applaud her for it!" he yelled. "And if Mo's alone she deserves to be. That girl is sneaky as fuck and you don't see it."

"She's my cousin, Wisdom!"

"And I'm your man!" He backed away and blinked a few times. "Hold up, so that's why you wanted to have nasty sex? On the bar? To butter me up for this shit?"

"It's not like that…you know what happened."

"You mean she's still holding that rape over your head?" He said a little louder. "Because you and I both know Carter never would've fucked her unless she gave him the go 'head. The man doing time right now behind her lies."

"My cousin wouldn't lie about no shit like that!" I said raising my voice. It was the first time I ever had and it felt good. "I don't talk about your family so don't talk about mine."

"She's a whore, Carlita. One minute she's at the bar drinking with him. Five different niggas and two bitches said they heard her telling him about all the things she wanted to do later that night. They leave out. *Together*. And the next thing you know she's yelling rape." He paused. "You might not want to hear it but she's a liar and a slut."

I exhaled. "You have your opinion and you know I love you but you're wrong, Wisdom. And I'm only giving her six months." I walked up to him and wrapped my arms around his waist and rested my head against the top of his stomach. He felt like a stiff piece of plywood. "Please hang in there with me."

"Be on the lookout," Poe yelled rushing into the bar.

I separated from Wisdom and looked at Poe. "What's going on?"

"My man said some niggas threatening to shoot up the spot again. Asking questions about Monique and shit like that. So keep your eyes peeled for anything suspicious."

Wisdom removed a gun from underneath the counter that I didn't know was there. He cocked and loaded it. "Don't even worry, playboy. We good back here."

I realized then I don't know my boyfriend. At all.

CHAPTER EIGHT

SPYRELLA

I wiped sweat off of my brow after mowing half of the lawn. Why I'm doing this when I'm not going to be around long, I really don't know.

The white t-shirt I'm wearing clings to my sweaty body and my blue jeans look like I pissed in them. I wanted the yard to be nice since my intention was to burn the house to the ground.

I also didn't expect to be so lonely so I wanted to keep busy. Mo may have been mean and Carlita may have thought about me as a charity project but at least we all lived together.

I was just about to start the lawn mower again when a large green dumpster truck pulled in front of my house. It was the Department of Sanitation. Luckily I placed the trashcans on the side of the house so I didn't have to run in and get them. I bought new sheets, dishes and a lot of other things so the cans were loaded with trash.

I turned the lawn mower on and caught a glimpse of a 6-foot something, chocolate man. He hopped out of the passenger side and moved toward the cans. He wore a plain white t-shirt and large gloves, and a long sleeve work shirt was tied around his waist. His beard was nice and he was chubby, also a plus. When I realized he was probably off limits and out of my league I started mowing.

From the corner of my eyes I watched him dump the first can and the next. I felt like he was watching me but I turned away when I realized for what. He had zero reason to be checking me out. I just finished one row of mowing when I turned around again and he was standing behind me.

I looked up at him. "Is everything okay?" I backed away and tugged on my wet t-shirt to let in some air. "Was I supposed to put the cans somewhere else?"

He smiled. "Why you doing this?"

I wiped the sweat off my brow with the back of my hand and looked at the ground. He was confusing. "It needed to be done." I shrugged. "Don't want to find dead animals in my grass."

He smiled. "I mean where's your man?"

"Don't need a man to do this kind of stuff, anybody can do it."

"So you don't have one, or you avoiding the question?"

"Come on, Reggie," his coworker yelled. "We got the whole block! I'm not trying to be out here all day!"

Reggie turned around and put one finger up before turning back to me. "I gotta go before I kill my co-worker." He paused. "But let me take you out and I promise…I won't hurt you."

He won't hurt me?

That's a weird thing to say.

I could feel my heart beating fast and thought I would pass out. I can't remember the last time somebody asked me on a date. Oh I remember now, never. "I know…wish I could but…I'm not sure if…no. I can't. I'm sorry."

"So you gonna play hard to get when you know I want you?"

I looked down at my body and was disgusted. I didn't know what he saw in me but I felt it was sexual. "I'm in a relationship, so if you don't mind I have a lot to do around here." I turned the mower back on and pushed it away from him.

A few seconds later I heard him laughing behind my back. "You know the messed up part?" He yelled to be heard over the mower.

"What's that?" I said never taking my eyes off the grass.

"The messed up part is that you don't even know you just shot down your husband. I'm not worried though. Ten years from now we're going to be posted up in our home and I'll tell our kids all about it." He walked toward the truck, got inside and it pulled off.

Reggie's eyes remained on me the whole time.

I sat in Mama's Kitchen Soul Food restaurant and stuffed my face with a mound of pancakes. I had already finished a plate of home fries and was ready to start on my fried chicken when my stomach bubbled. This was my last meal since I decided tonight I would take my life.

And since my mother let me down, by not coming to the house, I figured I'd have to do it alone.

After putting a pile of paper towels on the toilet in the bathroom I plopped down on the seat when I heard someone throwing up in the stall next to me. I started to ask if she was okay but what was I going to do? I was in the bathroom next to her and couldn't help.

After I finished and flushed the toilet, I walked to the sink to wash my hands and I still heard her vomiting so hard I thought she would cough up her lungs. I was about to knock on the stall door when she came out, wiping the corners of her mouth with her finger. "Are you okay?" I asked.

She was a pretty brown girl who was skin and bones. She looked at me, shook her head and laughed. "Don't look so scared," she said. She walked to the sink, turned on the water and looked at me again. "If you must know I was purging."

She was rude and I probably should've left but I was intrigued. "What's purging?"

She rolled her eyes, washed her hands and turned off the water. "Let's just say judging by your size, you should do it too. It might save your life. As big as you are you must be miserable."

CHAPTER NINE

MONIQUE

The thump of the stereo system rattled my heart even as I sat in my dressing room preparing to dance at Skeezers for the first night since the renovations. There were so many red roses in my room, the smell overpowering but it was beautiful to look at. Poe outdid himself and sometimes I get the impression he was leading me on. Pulling me with him but never close enough to be his woman. The worst part was I'm too weak to do anything about it.

As I glanced at myself in the mirror, I looked up at Poe who was standing behind me. "Nervous?" he asked placing his hands on my shoulders. He did that a lot and I loved it. "Because you don't need to be. I have every bit of faith that you're going to murder the game as usual."

"You're right, this isn't my first rodeo but it does feel good hearing that you believe in me." I grabbed my red lipstick in the gold container. "It's like riding a bike." I covered my lips with the vibrant color, puckered up and blew him a kiss. "I just hope I make you proud. So you know you can always count on me. You know that right, Poe?"

"You haven't showed me any different." He exhaled. "Levine said we have a full house tonight. Wanted me to put her in the line-up and everything." He laughed. "But I told her to let the young girls have at it."

I shook my head. "You can't fault my mother for trying."

"I know, but I need her to get the new girls together. I know she's upset she won't get the paper she use to but I'm still looking out."

"My mother will be okay." I waved. "I take care of her every month."

"You heard about some niggas sliding past here earlier? Looking for you?"

I tried to hold my laughter. I had my friend Waxton bring his cousins by with hoodies to pump fear into Poe. I never wanted him to think I was safe. I wanted him to always assume that without him I could get hurt, mainly because he was in the *save a woman* business.

"I heard, Carlita told me. And I'm not gonna lie, I was scared." I am lying.

"I don't want you worrying about shit. I got five of my niggas on the door inside and five more outside. I'm not sure what the drama was about but you're safe in here and you're safe with me." He exhaled. "Enough of that, the Baltimore promoter we used made sure every nigga worth a million is in the building. I wouldn't be surprised if you cleared a hundred thou."

I felt an electric current shoot through me just thinking about the possibilities. "Really? You think it's gonna be that kind of night?"

"I'm positive, Mo. Everything is perfect. Truth be told all you gotta do is go get your money."

I looked down and sighed. "Things are almost perfect," I said standing up, walking toward the glittery coat rack.

"What's wrong now?" He sat on the sofa and ran one hand down his face in frustration. "Why aren't you happy?"

"Poe, can I ask you something and trust that you'll tell me the truth?" I removed the velvet robe covering my body and placed it on the rack, revealing the silver costume underneath. I had it custom-made and it fit my body perfectly. "I want to know the truth even if you think it will hurt."

"I'll always be honest with you." His eyes roamed from my feet to my breasts, before slowly crawling to my face.

"Are you gay?"

Before I knew it he was off the sofa and in my face, staring down at me, his hot breath spreading across my forehead. "What did you just say to me?"

"Are you gay?"

"What would make you think some shit like that?" He yelled.

"Because you don't want me."

He exhaled, turned around and ran his hand over his face again. "You are the most arrogant chick I've ever met in my life. Just because you got niggas eating out of your palm and I'm not one of them, you question my sexuality?"

"I just don't understand what it is and it doesn't have anything to do with other guys. Although I would understand why you didn't want me if I was as big as Spy's funky ass."

He laughed sarcastically although I didn't catch the joke.

"Poe, I'm serious. I can tell you think I'm attractive because even now you can't keep your eyes off me. But what I don't get is why you don't give me a chance. What is the real reason you don't want Mo?" I yelled slapping myself on my phat ass. Without even looking down I could feel it jiggle.

He looked at me and laughed. "I'll answer part of the question, because we don't have time for the rest. One of the reasons I don't want you is because every time I think something is there, every time I feel myself wondering what it would be like to make you mine, you remind me of how vicious you can be. I own a strip club." He nodded. "I understand that I will never be a prophet or someone respected but what I do have is heart. And I don't go around trying to make people feel bad because I have power."

"Poe, it's not—"

He raised his hand. "Monique, we're business partners." His voice low and his words slow. "Nothing more and nothing less." He walked toward the door. "Now hurry up. You on the clock."

Hanging on the top of the pole I was in the middle of a money tornado. There were so many bills floating around me that I couldn't see anybody, not even Poe.

I thought about what he said about me being vicious and although I didn't agree with him, I understood where he was coming from. Part of the reason I loved Poe so much was that he was considerate. He was the sugar to my black coffee, no cream. So although I knew I couldn't be extra soft like he wanted, I was an actress. And I knew how to apologize.

In my own way of course.

When the end of the Fetty Wap song went off I slid down, readying myself for the next part of my plan. Poe could resist me but he couldn't resist his favorite song *"How Can I Love U 2nite"* by *Sisqo*. The moment the song came on I saw Poe turn around and look at the stage. He was talking to Julio and Curtis from Uptown but now he was staring at me.

When Sisqo's voice pumped out he shook his head and gave me a sly look as I begin to move my body like a snake. He walked backwards and plopped down in a chair, as if already taken in by my spell.

And to think, I didn't do anything yet.

With mini dance moves in between, I stepped off the stage and slowly made my way toward Poe. Every step was deliberate and calculating and I realized it could all go wrong. He wasn't one for public displays of affection but I was taking a chance.

When I was standing in front of him I winked and wiggled softly and slowly, careful to keep my distance. He shook his head again and said, "You something else you know that?"

I had him.

I turned around and slowly sat on his lap just as Sisqo sung, *'Don't cum, baby please wait for me, just think how wet we're gonna be.'* I smiled at the customers who now circled the chair and tossed more bills in the air. There wasn't a space on the floor visible. I moved and grinded until I felt his stiffness against the seat of my ass.

Now I really got him.

When the song was over I turned around and looked at him, still sitting on his lap, the heat from my pussy against his dick. "You tired of playing games as much as I am?"

"Mo, not here."

I placed my index finger on his lips. I lowered my head and whispered in his ear. "No more games, Poe. I'm yours and you're mine. Now come get this pussy."

He lifted me up and my legs wrapped around his waist. Arms on his shoulders while he gripped my ass, he looked into my eyes. "I hope I'm not making a mistake."

"How can you make a mistake when love is involved?" He walked me to my dressing room.

The moment the door opened and closed he stuck his tongue into my mouth, snatched off my outfit and sat me on the edge of the vanity. Within seconds I felt his hard dick stabbing inside of me. "This what you wanted, bitch?" He said as he banged into me like a wild animal.

"Ye…ye…yes," I stuttered, my body jerking up and down.

"You wanted this dick and you gonna get it now." He fucked me so hard it was borderline painful. "Still think I'm gay, bitch? I should've smacked the shit out of your ass for disrespecting me."

I couldn't speak, every inch of my body tingled and since I waited so long for this moment I was about to cum. When I felt his penis throbbing I knew he was about to let go to and within seconds he came.

I really got him now and mama would be so proud.

CHAPTER TEN

SPYRELLA

ONE MONTH LATER

I took the last wing from the hot grease and placed it on the paper towel. When I looked out of the window over the stove I noticed snow was falling heavily, I almost couldn't see across the street to the next house. The weather was supposed to be bad and I was trying to prepare everything for my company so that tonight would be perfect.

When there was a knock at the door I wiped my hand on my strawberry apron and walked toward it. He's early but I wasn't concerned because the food wouldn't take much longer. When I looked out the peephole I was surprised to see my mother. Smiling I let her in. "Ma?" She still looked like she was living on the streets. "What are you doing here?"

She looked me up and down as snow fell on the top of her head, making her old braids brown and white. "Spyrella, you lost…you lost so much weight." She smiled. "I mean how did you do it?"

I glanced down at myself, temporarily forgetting that I was smaller than the last time she saw me. "Yeah…I've been working at it. Have a long way to go though."

She laughed. "Working at it? You have to be at least fifty pounds lighter."

I cleared my throat. "Just watching what I eat and stuff like that." I stepped back and opened the door wider. "Come inside, ma. You'll catch a cold out there."

She dusted the fresh snow off of her head and clothes and walked in, her jaw dropping as she looked around. I'm sure she's shocked at how beautiful my house is. It's not like she's been here but even I was amazed at how much love I placed into the house. After all the plan was to stay here for some months, eat as much as I want and then take my life. Honestly I'm not one hundred percent sure that plan is not off the board. But when I first got here I didn't see any way out of my grief.

Things are slightly different now.

"Did this house come like this?" She asked, glancing around.

"Not really. It was pretty bare. I installed the recess lighting, painted the living room yam, my bathroom soft blue and my bedroom eggshell color."

She looked over at me. "The same colors in our old house." She swallowed. "The one I burned down."

I nodded. I hadn't realized I'd done that.

"Well it really is beautiful and comfortable." She tossed her black backpack on the floor. She removed her gloves and coat and tossed them on the floor. My mother had a tendency to be nasty, even when I was a kid so I guess not a lot had changed.

"I'm still working on some things but for now it'll do." I picked her coat and gloves up and put them on the chair. "What are you doing here, ma?"

She sighed. "I've decided to take you up on your offer. And move in with you." She paused. "That is if you still need me."

"It's been a little over a month, some things have changed."

She nodded. "What was so important anyway?"

I was going to kill myself.

"Nothing you needed to worry about." I waved her off. "Was having an identity crisis that's all." I exhaled. "But I am happy that you're here, ma and you're welcome to stay as long as you like. I have plenty of room."

She hugged me and I inhaled for a moment the elements of the street that was all over her clothing and skin. "Ma, how about you go take a shower and put on some clean clothes. Afterwards I'll make you a plate."

"Am I intruding?" she paused and gazed at the candles I set up around the living room. "Looks like you're waiting for someone else."

"It'll be fine, ma. I want you here, so please don't worry about it." I smiled again. "Come with me." I walked her to the guest bathroom and handed her some sweat pants and a white t-shirt from my room. "The soap is under the sink and a washcloth and towel are in the cabinet over the—" The doorbell rang and interrupted my thought.

"Your company is here," She smiled, her teeth as yellow as lemons. "I'll be fine."

"Okay, let me know if you need anything."

I rushed toward the front door, leaving my mother where she was. I didn't mean to go so abruptly but I was expecting company. When I opened the door Reggie was on the other side holding a bouquet of red roses speckled with snow. He was wearing blue jeans and I could smell the leather from his black jacket. "You're beautiful." He kissed me on the cheek and I pulled his cold hand inside.

After kissing I placed the flowers in a vase and walked him to the dining room where I prepared his plate. We had been dating for a month and I loved the time and attention he showed me. These days I was not alone.

But there was one problem.

Reggie didn't like my weight loss goals. He wanted me fat but I was uncomfortable. I had always been a thin girl trapped in a fat girl's body and although I tried to convince him that the only reason I gave him a chance was because I loved the new body I was building, he didn't seem happy. In the end he told me he would support my change but I got the impression it wasn't the case.

"My mom's here," I said under my breath.

His eyes widened. "That's good, baby. You said you'd been looking for her." He paused. "So how come you don't look happy?"

"I am...it's just that...I guess I wasn't expecting her."

"So how long will she be here?"

"I think she's gonna be here for a while." I ate my biscuit and downed it with some water. "You don't mind do you?"

He looked shocked. "Spy, I would never come between you and your mother. I'm looking forward to meeting her."

"Really?" I asked with wide eyes.

"If she's a part of you I want the best for you."

I got up, downed the rest of the water in my glass and kissed him on the cheek. "That's why I love you." He smacked me in the ass. "I'm going to the bathroom. My mom's in the guest one so I have to go to my room."

"Cool, I'll open the wine."

"Okay." I rushed upstairs. When I was in my bathroom I closed the door and grabbed my red toothbrush. On my knees in front of the toilet I stuck the bottom of the toothbrush down my throat and vomited as quietly as possible. I had been doing it so long it was easy.

I almost finished purging when the door flung open and Reggie was standing in the doorway holding two glasses of wine. "Baby, I poured you a—" When he saw me on the floor he placed both glasses on the sink and walked deeper inside. His face was pulled into a frown and he looked like he wanted to hurt me. "Yo, what the fuck you doing?"

I stood up, flushed the toilet and wiped my mouth with the back of my hand. Trying to think of a good lie I moved to the sink. "I wasn't feeling well." I turned the water on, rinsed my toothbrush and brushed my teeth.

"You doing it again aren't you?" He crossed his arms over his chest. "You promised me you wasn't but you still are."

"Reggie, I told you I don't feel well."

"STOP FUCKING LYING TO ME!"

I jumped at the sound of his voice. "Reggie, I know how it looks, but I promise I'm done with that." I rinsed my mouth and turned the water off.

"Let me be clear, I will not deal with a woman who abuses her body. Ever!"

"And being fat is not an abuse?"

"I'm serious!" he pointed in my face. "You said you wanted to lose weight and I got behind that because I'm trying to get to know you even though I like my women big. But if I find out you throwing up to be a size I'm not even feeling, I won't fuck with you anymore! I hope you prepared to deal with that." When he turned around my mother was standing there. He wiped his hand down his face and said, "Uh…hey…it's nice to meet you." He walked around her and stomped down the stairs.

CHAPTER ELEVEN
CARLITA

"She doesn't want that kind of hair, she says it has to be without the cuticles attached."

I was frustrated with the attendant at the beauty supply store because I had Monique on the cell phone screaming in my ear and Wisdom at my side. Earlier I convinced him that our planned trip to the grocery store wouldn't be sidetracked too long with a stop for Mo.

That was two hours ago and we haven't been to the food store yet.

"I'm telling you brand you seek doesn't come with cuticles attached." The Asian woman seemed at her wits end with me. "If it did I would sell! I'm in business of money. You sure friend has right brand?"

"Tell that bitch I've been coming there for two years and I know what hair I used. It's *May Black Brazilia*n hair with the cuticles."

I sighed and looked over at Wisdom. "I'll be in the car," he said before storming off.

Now we gonna be fighting all day behind this shit.

"They don't have it, Monique." I rolled my eyes. "Did you want anything else? I had some place else to be."

"You know what, just bring the *May Black* brand with cuticles. I'll look for it myself later. Of course thanks to you I got to pay Waxton $300.00 for a weave job with some fucked up hair!"

I didn't feel like arguing. My man was in the car mad about it all and she already ruined my day. I looked at the attendant. "She said give me the May Black." The attendant rolled her eyes and packaged the order. I handed her money and grabbed my change. "Got the hair, I'll see you later, Monique."

"Come to Skeezers, I'm having my hair done here to be ready for my set tonight."

I frowned. "But you said bring it to the house! I got Wisdom with me and he gonna be madder if we gotta go out the way to the club."

"But I ain't there! Plus the more time you spend on the phone…"

I can't with this bitch!

"Okay, Mo." I hung up on her and walked toward my car. After everything I went through just now it irritated me more that she didn't even say thank you.

I'm not her fucking maid! I'm her cousin and I'm tired of being used.

Once I got in the car I tossed the hair in the back and got behind the steering wheel. "You want to buy something to eat?"

"No," Wisdom said as he strolled through his cell phone. He didn't bother to look up at me.

"I thought we were going out?" I pulled the car into traffic.

"We were supposed to cook remember? This trip was only supposed to take five minutes remember?" he laughed sarcastically. "For real, all I want to do is go home. I'll find us something to eat at the house. I bought some steaks last week, figured I'll throw some potatoes in the oven and get some asparagus."

I smiled because if he thought this much about dinner it meant he wasn't *that* mad. "Okay, I have to drop the hair off at Skeezers and then we can—"

"I've gone through the process already to buy the house." He stuffed his cell into his pocket. "I got it and I'm moving in a week. It's what I wanted to talk to you about."

I felt like I was about to shit on myself and pulled the car to the side of the road. I moved my body to look into his eyes. "Wisdom, I thought we were…doing it together?"

"I'm not waiting no more, Carlita. I can't sit by while you let this chick run your life. Either you're with me or you're not. Looks like you already chose. I just hope you made the right decision."

"Wisdom, don't do this. I told you that she's afraid to be alone and you said you would wait. It's only been a month."

"Did you hear how that bitch talked to you back there…in the store? Huh? Its one thing to live with her but it's a whole 'notha thing to let her run your life. I'm done with sitting by and watching this shit. I gotta move on."

Warm tears ran down my cheeks. "When are you moving?"

"A week and if you're not with me when I get the keys it's over, Carlita. I'm washing my hands of you."

I walked into Monique's dressing room and Waxton was braiding her hair for the weave. When Mo saw me she said, "Girl, I thought I was gonna have to cuss your ass out." She reached out. "Give me the hair so I can get this shit done."

I handed it to her and looked at Waxton, her closest friend and hairdresser. He was gay, loud and as mean as she was so for real I didn't like him. "You mind giving us five minutes alone?"

He rolled his eyes and looked down at Monique. "You want me to go?"

"Yeah, it's okay."

"Well hurry up because I'm not gonna be here all day. Got another appointment later tonight." He bumped me on his way out.

"I can't stand him," I said through my teeth.

"He's cool but you know how he is." She looked in my eyes. "Oh shit, what did Wisdom do now?"

"He's moving in the new house in a week."

"That's good. So what he gonna do, get things ready for you to come in five months?"

"No, he wants me to help him plan and I'm going sooner. I gotta save my relationship, Mo and I hope you understand."

She tossed the hair on her dresser. "So what you saying?"

"I'm moving out. I can't lose Wisdom." I moved closer, pulled up a chair and sat in front of her. "Lately I've had a feeling that he's been pulling away. I even saw him keeping time with white girl Ohio the other day."

"I knew he wasn't shit." She slapped her hands together. "If you ask me that should be more of a reason for you to leave him alone."

"But I'm not gonna leave him alone and I'm not gonna hand my nigga over to another chick either. I have to make things work and I'm willing to do anything."

She exhaled, looked down at her hands that were clutched in her lap and back at me. "I'm not mad, Carlita. Wisdom is a good man and I can understand you wanting to spend the rest of your life with him. I guess jealousy had me being selfish and not thinking of you." She scooted toward me and placed her hand over mine. "It's okay. Go and be with him. I'm just gonna have to find another roommate."

My eyes widened. "Are you serious?"

"I'm positive." She hugged me and I inhaled her perfume. "We'll be okay, you'll see."

I was surprised. She sounded sincerely happy for me. I just wish I could believe her."

CHAPTER TWELVE
MONIQUE

"You know I'm not saying that, Poe. I just wouldn't have done it to her is all." I placed my seat belt on as he pulled out of the parking lot. "She's my cousin and I'm done with her."

"You shouldn't cut her off just because she wants to be with Wisdom. It's not like you need her to pay the rent. Your house is paid off already. Been paid off for years."

"But they didn't know that."

He looked over at me. "So you were pocketing the money that Carlita gave you for rent?"

"Pocketing the money?" I laughed. "I paid that house off a long time ago. Just because I'm making a little back by charging Carlita rent doesn't make me a villain."

He laughed. "You cold."

"It's not that, I just…I mean…"

"Maybe she's leaving for the same reason Spy left because of how you treat people." He cut his left blinker on and merged over. "If you don't be careful everybody you love gonna be gone."

"Is that a threat?"

"I would never threaten you."

"That's the only thing I don't like about you, Poe. No matter what I do you always imagine me as this monster. And it's so far from who I am. To have known me for so many years I would think you would know my heart." I shook my head. "That's fucked up and it hurts."

"Let's drop it."

I looked at him from the corner of my eye. I didn't want to drop it. I wanted to talk more but he hated to be pushed. "What you doing tonight?"

"Nothing. You know we have that NBA party tomorrow at the club so I have a lot to take care of." He looked at me. "You can stay over tonight if you want but I have a few more stops to make. I should be back early though."

"Can I ask you something without you getting mad?" I paused. "Because something's been on my mind."

He sighed. "Go 'head, Mo."

"How do you feel about our relationship so far? Do you think we're coming along?"

"Like I said a few days ago I think we should take it slow. Let's not gauge shit every week. We've been friends for so long that we have to be careful."

"Well what do you think about me staying with you? With Carlita moving out I'm alone. And I've never been alone in my life." I wiped my sweaty palms on my jeans. "Do you think that you…I mean…could…"

"What, Mo?"

"Let me live with you? I promise to stay out of your way if—"

I stopped talking because he was shaking his head no even though I didn't finish talking. "We just started seeing each other, Mo. Why would you jump into a living situation so soon?"

"I just told you why."

"You're a woman and you shouldn't be afraid to stay by yourself for something that happened years ago. You have to move on. Plenty of women were raped and are stronger."

I felt my body trembling because even now when I needed him he was only willing to give me part of him.

I wanted him to be fully present and step up now more than ever. "So you won't let me stay with you? Not even until I'm use to living alone?"

He looked over at me and exhaled. "I don't think it will be a good idea. I got a lot of shit going on right now and the last thing I want to do is take it out on you. I'm sorry."

Even though he said I could stay over tonight, I decided to stay at my place anyway. I felt sick to my stomach every time I thought about how he treated me. If he didn't want me around I decided not to stay around. The thing was I forgot how much the house seemed to moan when I was alone. Everywhere I turned there was a crack or bump and I believed in my heart that somebody was in here waiting to hurt me.

When there was a knock on my door I almost jumped out of my skin until I remembered I asked Waxton over. I grabbed the comforter that I had wrapped around my body and walked to the front door to let him in. The moment Waxton came inside I hugged him and locked the door.

"What's wrong with you girl?" he looked around. "You act like I'm about to give you some pussy or something."

"First of all you don't have a pussy and second of all I'm just happy to see you."

He looked around. "Why? What the fuck is going on?"

I pulled him toward the sofa and he sat down. "I think somebody's in my house."

He jumped up. "What you mean somebody in the house?" He looked around again. "Call the fucking police!"

"I can't, it's difficult to explain."

He frowned and backed away. "Well unless you want me to leave this bitch you better tell me something."

He hadn't bothered to sit back down and since I needed him to hang around for a minute I decided to be real. "I've called the police before when I heard noises. They came in and nobody was here." I exhaled. "Actually five different times they came and they couldn't find anybody. They said one more time and I would be fined."

He placed his fingers on his chin. "So wait...you call the police and lie?"

I frowned. "I'm not lying, somebody is in here."

"Okay, girl, this is too much. How about you tell me why I'm here so I can go on with my life." He looked around again and back at me. "Because now you got me hearing things."

"Okay, okay, I need you to do me a favor and you can't back out."

"Is this a paying favor? Because I can't be bothered with you these days about my money. My cousins still mad about you saying you were gonna pay one fee and gave me something else. Splitting five hundred dollars between three niggas not enough."

"All they had to do was drive up and scare Poe in front of Skeezers! Who said they needed three people?" I paused. "Anyway this job is paying but I need it done A.S.A.P."

He smiled. "Bitch, as long as I'm getting my money the skies are the limit." He finally sat down. "Now tell me what you need."

CHAPTER THIRTEEN

SPYRELLA

ONE MONTH LATER

I had five more minutes on the treadmill after running for an hour. Sweat drops were sprinkled everywhere and I loved it. The past few months I felt light on my feet and my endurance was way up. If only I could get Reggie, who now lived with me, to stop making foods that do nothing but make me feel guilty after I stuff my face. Sometimes I feel like he wants me fat on purpose although he tells me it's not true.

My mother walked up on me and she seemed worried. "I have a few runs to make, Spy but do you mind if I talk to you for a moment, in private?" These days she looked like an entirely different person and even got a job as a waitress at a diner around the corner. Her life was coming along but she always seemed like there was something on her mind. Something she didn't trust me enough to understand.

"Uh, sure." I wiped my face with the purple towel on the treadmill and walked toward the den that was directly off the living room. When we were alone I sat on the arm of the chair. "What's up?"

"I'm worried about you, Spy. Very worried."

My jaw dropped. "Wait, I have never been happier and thinner and you're worried about me?" I pointed to myself.

"I hear you in the bathroom when Reggie's at work," she whispered "I hear you throwing up."

I felt dizzy because after Reggie caught me the last time I did my best to hide the secret from him, making sure to only do it when he wasn't home. "Ma, you can't tell him," I said in a low voice. "You can't let him know."

"Spy, I never told you this because I was afraid you wouldn't be able to handle it. But when I was growing up I wanted to be a dancer too. More than anything. That's where you got it from." She smiled. "I was good at it. So good I was getting recruited to some of the best colleges in the world. My dream was to go to New York and make it big." She sighed. "I had a boyfriend at the time and I loved him a lot. More than anything. And the plan was for him to go with me."

"Did he?"

"I came home early one day, after visiting Julliard. When I did I saw Levine and him, sitting in the car out front of our house, having sex." She sighed and I saw tears flow down her face. "They ended up being together for awhile and it tore me apart. I never recovered."

"I'm sorry, ma."

She wiped tears away. "It's okay. Really." She exhaled. "Levine had always been sexual and I thought if I could be like her, move like her, that he would want me too." She paused. "Well he didn't want me. But I spent a lot of time trying to be someone that I wasn't. And look at the condition of my life, Spy." She got up and placed her hand on mine. "Don't trade places with me. Don't be someone you aren't. It'll kill you in the long run." She stood up, kissed me and walked out.

My mother never shared her story with me before but that was her business not mine. I didn't want to be like anyone but myself and as far as I'm concerned she could kiss my ass. The new me was improved and I was not gonna stop doing what I was to look good.

When I walked into the kitchen I saw Reggie was making French fries while a big pitcher of lemonade sat on the counter. I walked up behind him and he winked at me. "The lemonade is on point if you want some."

"Nope, I think I'll get some water." I opened the fridge, grabbed a bottle of Fiji and gulped it down.

"But you love my lemonade." He reached into the cabinet over my head and poured me a large glass anyway. It was so full that juice oozed from the sides.

I looked at it and frowned. "Reggie, I said I don't want it."

He placed it on the table. "Let me ask you something, are you going to let this weight loss change who you are?" He paused. "Because for one week when we first got together you were so happy. And now…well now things are different."

"Change who I am? For your information I was small before you met me, Reggie. And I was miserable when I was fat." I pushed the lemonade aside. "Just because you have some fat girl fetish doesn't mean I have to be a part of it."

"Fat girl fetish?" He frowned and turned off the hot grease. "If a man wanted to date only white women, or light skin women, no one would say he had a fetish. But because I like big women I'm some kind of freak now?"

"I'm not saying that."

"Then what are you saying, Spy? That I'm wrong for loving you how I met you and that I want you to be the same?" He walked up to me and grabbed me around my waist. I started to resist because I was sweaty but I knew he wouldn't care. He once ate my pussy after I cleaned the house all day and was dripping with perspiration. "I want you as you were and there will be nothing you can say to convince me that I'm wrong for feeling that way."

"I know, Reggie, and I love that about you. But you must understand that unless I'm a size I'm comfortable with, I will never be truly happy. Ever."

To get my mind off of things Reggie invited me to the movies to see the new Denzel Washington flick. And to make him feel like I appreciated the gesture I ordered a hot dog, popcorn, candy and water.

While he was paying for the food two dudes kept looking at me and at first I thought they were staring at someone behind me. That is until the taller of the two walked up to me. "I'm not trying to be disrespectful but I just had to say you were beautiful."

My jaw hung because I hadn't received a compliment from anyone but Reggie and Poe in a year. "Thank...thank you. I...appreciate it." I tried not to blush but the attention made me feel good.

"Are you taken?" he continued.

Reggie suddenly put his arm around my shoulder and said, "She is." He extended his hand and the tallest one shook it. "We appreciate the compliment."

The tallest one said, "No disrespect, man. She is bad though." Both of them walked away.

"That was crazy," I said to Reggie who didn't seem to impressed."

"They just niggas." He waved them off.

When we got inside the theater the previews were playing. He seemed a little distant after the compliment and I hoped he wasn't mad at me. "Are you okay, Reggie?"

He looked at me and squeezed my chin softly. "Why wouldn't I be?"

The theater got darker and I could feel the tension growing. Almost like he was going to do something although I didn't know what. Since the previews were still on we made small talk and then he floored me.

"I don't want to be with anybody else in this world, Spy. Anybody. Can you see being with me only? Forever?"

"Yeah, I think so."

"I need you to know."

"Of course, Reggie. There's nobody else." He winked and to avoid talking anymore I downed my hotdog, candy, popcorn and water. When I was done I said, "I'll be right back. I have to go to the lady's room."

He smiled and I rushed to the bathroom so I wouldn't miss the movie. Once in the stall I stuck my finger down my throat and threw up everything I ate. I could feel a flap of skin in my throat swell up but I didn't care. After the attention I got there was nothing going to stop me from being thin and this worked for me. In my mind I was getting the best of both worlds.

When I came out of the stall this fat bitch standing in front of the sink stared at me like I was crazy. She reminded me of myself back in the day and I felt I had to give her the best advice given to me. "You need to purge, honey. And if you don't know what that means I suggest you look it up."

When I was done I went back in the theater and enjoyed the movie with Reggie. He acted like something was still on his mind and I figured it was the guy who tried to talk to me until we were in the car going home.

Instead of driving to the house he pulled on the side of the road. Grabbing one of my hands he exhaled and looking into my eyes. "I know I've been weird all night. I wanted to do this earlier but it seemed like something kept coming up. I knew if I didn't do it now it'll never happen."

"What's going on, Reggie?"

"Shhhh." He placed a finger over his lips. "I love you, Spy. I've never loved anybody the way I do you. And I know it's early but I'm asking you and begging you, to be my wife."

My jaw hung. "What…I…I…"

"You deserve to be happy and if you allow me I can do that for you. We live together, we love each other, what do we have to lose?"

I looked at him and thought about our lives. He cooked for me. Worked hard for me and I barely had to lift a finger. For the first time in my life, in a crazy shift, I was the one being catered to. I may have had a few dudes looking my way but it was Reggie who kept me safe and warm. It was Reggie who sincerely wanted me even if I got fat again.

What did I have to lose?

"Yes," I said. "Yes I will be your wife."

He shot his fists up in the air and hugged me excitedly, like he just won high stakes in a football game. "You see, I told you that you'd never get away from me. And I was right."

CHAPTER FOURTEEN

MONIQUE

I placed the last bit of makeup on my face in my dressing room and was getting ready to do my set when Wisdom busted inside. "Boy, what's wrong with you? Why you coming in here all crazy?" I frowned.

"The cops, they're outside of the club asking for you. Wouldn't tell me what was happening but it looks serious. I'm closing the club, go see what they want."

I jumped up and rushed to the front door. Customers were leaving, I guess none of them wanted to be questioned by the police. When I was in the front of the club I stood in front of three officers – one black and two white. "Can I help you with something?" I folded my arms over my chest. "I mean is everything okay?"

"Ma'am, do you have any clothing to put on?" The black police officer said. "This is a serious matter."

"I don't have anything that covers me more than this." I looked down at my black bra and panty set. "So let's make it quick, what's happening."

He exhaled. "Do you live off of Barryman Road? In Washington DC?"

"Yes," I said eyes alternating between all of them. "What's happening?"

"It's been burned," he said with heavy breath. "I'm sorry to tell you this but we need to take some information from you."

I collapsed and unbeknownst to me Wisdom was behind me to help me up. "Is my whole house gone?" I placed my fingers over my mouth.

"I'm afraid so mam," he said softly. "Are you alright?" He reached out to help me but I was already stable.

I nodded yes.

"Is...anything left?"

"No, everything is gone." He paused. "Do you know who may be responsible for something like this?" He grabbed a pen and notebook from his front pocket.

I looked into the sky, although I could answer his question without needing to think. Lately my plans needed plans and I hoped this was the last one I would have to change. "The only person I can think of is my aunt Diane. Spyrella's mother."

"You sure about that?" Wisdom asked. I forgot he was behind me.

"I wouldn't have said it, if I wasn't sure." I rolled my eyes.

The officer recorded my notes. "So Spyrella is your cousin?"

"Yes."

"Do you know where she lives?"

"She moved from the house we shared months ago. And the last time I heard my aunt was living on the street, at the park. Not sure if she still is because of the weather and all."

The cops stayed a little longer and recorded more information. I gave them everything I wanted them to have and when I was done they left. Relieved, I decided my work wasn't done.

Since all of the customers were gone I called Poe and told him what happened. "I'm so sorry, Mo. I really am. I'll catch the next flight back tomorrow." He paused. "You can stay with me until we figure all this out. Don't worry about a thing."

I got him again!

Guess I'm living with him after all.

He was in LA and couldn't be here but called repeatedly to make sure I was okay. He also told me where his keys were so that I could let myself in and I knew in that moment I would never go home.

After everybody left Wisdom and I closed out the register. He was about to head out, I guess to be with Carlita, when I stopped him. "You think you can stay for a few minutes and have a drink with me? Please. I don't want to be alone."

Wisdom laughed so hard I thought he would fall over. "Yeah, right." He grabbed his book bag and car keys and walked around the counter.

"What's funny?" I frowned.

"You know you don't like me so let's not play games, Mo. You may have my girl fooled but I know all about you. And what kind of person you are. The last thing I need is to be is caught up on some bullshit."

He was about to walk out and I knew I had to kick things to the next level. So I busted out crying. Some people may find it hard to cry but for me it was easy. All of my life I felt like people hated me, or thought I was some evil monster when that couldn't be further from the truth. I'm a loving person who wants to be loved back and I'm willing to do whatever I can to make it happen.

To get my tears going I thought about Poe not wanting me. I thought about Spyrella and Carlita being selfish and leaving our home even though they knew I needed them. I thought about it all and suddenly the tears came easily.

Wisdom heard me, turned around, tossed his keys and book bag on the chair and walked up to me. I ran away, toward my dressing room. There was a reason for my madness and my show wouldn't be over until the end. "I'm sorry, Monique. I…I just thought you were fucking with me."

"No, go ahead, if you don't want to have a drink I understand." I walked inside my dressing room and he was on my heels. "I probably deserve everything I'm getting anyway."

"I'm sorry, Monique, I just thought that you were running game. I'll have a drink with you."

I snatched two tissues from the gold dispenser on the counter and wiped my tears. Then I blew my nose. "No, you don't have to."

"Monique, I said I will." His voice was firmer, like if I pushed it he would really leave. "What do you want me to fix us to drink?"

"Don't worry about it, I'll make it." I sniffled, rushing back to the bar. Once there I poured him a glass of Hennessey and myself vodka. Then I pulled the pills from under the cash register and plopped them into my drink. When I was finished I walked back into the dressing room and handed him his drink, while sipping slowly on mine.

An hour later he was on his third when suddenly I looked over at him and said, "Why don't you like me Wisdom? Why do you think I have anything but my cousin's best interests at heart."

"I'm her protector and if I see her upset then it'll make me have my own opinions about the person getting her that way."

I laughed. "You know, you a dumb nigger if you think my cousin won't run back to me in a few months. I hope you know that."

He placed the glass on the floor and blinked a few times. "Excuse me?"

"You heard me! Ever since we fucked, you been making it your life's work to separate me from my family. But if Carlita knew the things we use to do she wouldn't have anything to do with you."

"Wait, you blame me for not telling her? If I remember right you chose to keep our relationship a secret not me. I wanted to tell her and you begged me not to." He paused. "Now I wonder if it wasn't just so you could have something over my head."

"I told you not to tell her because our thing was before you and her got together. But I never knew you would pull this dumb shit either."

He laughed. "By dumb shit do you mean wanting my woman to be with me?" He shook his head. "Now I get it. You didn't want her to know because you're embarrassed that I dropped you. That I didn't want the relationship even though you did."

"Whatever."

"Ain't no whatever, bitch. You're miserable and you gonna be miserable long after I marry Carlita." He stood up. "I knew I shouldn't have stayed up in this bitch."

When he got up I jumped on him and pounded his back with my fists. It was important for me to keep my hands out of his face to serve my purpose. He tried to push me off but it didn't work and then suddenly he slapped me with his knuckles and my skin opened up like wet tissue. Blood was everywhere.

He busted my lips.

"Fuck!" he screamed. "Yo, Mo, I'm so sorry about this shit. I didn't mean for it to go this far, I just wanted you to leave me alone."

I looked at my face in the mirror and my white teeth were stained red. While he pleaded, I smiled. This looked way better than I could've imagined. He could apologize all he wanted because he gave me exactly what I needed.

Evidence.

I called the police and told them to hurry. And that Wisdom, my co-worker, tried to rape me.

And because of the drugs in my system I passed out.

CHAPTER FIFTEEN

CARLITA

As I drove erratically down the highway I couldn't understand what was happening in my life. One minute I was waiting for furniture movers in our new home and the next my fiancé was being arrested for raping my cousin.

I heard the "facts" from the police and I saw the picture with Monique's bloodied lip. Still none of this made sense. Wisdom could be a little bossy but he didn't have to rape anyone. Half of the strippers at Skeezers wanted him and at one point I thought Mo did too. But whenever I asked him, instead of him throwing her under the bus he would say, "You need to ask your cousin about that."

I never understood what he meant but I got the impression that she may have liked him. But rape? All this is so crazy.

My world came toppling down around me two days ago when Spy got a hold of me and told me my aunt Diane was arrested for burning down her house. My aunt didn't have a grudge against her as far as I knew so even that made limited sense. Had it not been for my aunt's record I would not have believed a thing.

When I finally made it to Poe's house I parked on the curb and rushed to the door. After knocking twice Poe opened it and gave me a hug. "Calm down, Carlita." He took my face into his warm hands and looked into my eyes. "Catch your breath, she's fine," He whispered. "I know it's hard but try not to be upset." He released my face and hugged me. I took a minute to cry in his arms because it was the first compassion I was shown by anyone since getting the news.

When I was a little relaxed I walked inside and he closed the door. Wiping my eyes with rough fists I stood in the middle of the foyer. "I don't understand, what's happening, Poe? You know Wisdom and you know he would never do anything like this? Right?"

He rubbed his hands down his face and stuffed them into his black slacks. "I wish I could tell you what's going on. I'm in LA helping my cousin with some business and the next thing I know I get a call that Mo's house is burned. And that Wisdom tried to rape her after drugging her."

"Drugging her?" I asked with widened eyes. "Wait a minute! He gave her something?"

"Yeah, the toxicology report came back this morning and she definitely had Rohypnol in her blood."

"What's that?"

"A rufi." He exhaled. "And since Wisdom been selling drugs since I've known him I— "

The room was spinning. "Hold up, you're saying that the man I love is a drug dealer?"

His eyes widened and I could see the guilt all over his face. Poe wasn't a snitching type dude and I could only assume that he thought I knew. "I'm so sorry, Carlita."

"For how long?"

"As long as I've known him." He shrugged. "I mean, he ain't moving no major weight but he does what he can to get by."

I thought about the times he would take money from me but never use it. His thing was my money was for the bank only. In the end every dime I ever gave him was in safekeeping. But a drug dealer? Who was he really? I felt sick to my stomach. "Where is she?" I placed my hand on my belly, trying to stop the queasiness.

"Upstairs." He moved closer. "But don't be surprised if she snaps on you, Carlita. She's been a handful lately and even though I care about her it's taking everything in my power not to walk away. I'm just preparing you."

"Please don't leave her, Poe. If you do she's all alone for real."

"I know but I can't...I don't..."

His words trailed off and I could tell he was holding back from saying more. "All I ask is that you don't make any crazy decisions now. Over the next few weeks she's gonna need us."

"The thing is, all of us still dealing with the rape at the club. Now another one happens. It's like we can't get out from under the dark cloud that follows her." He kissed me on the cheek and sighed. "I won't do anything right now, so don't worry. She's upstairs."

I walked up the steps and into the open door. Monique was lying on her side, faced the open window. Her back was in my direction and I sat on the edge of the bed. It squeaked a little. "Mo, it's me."

She turned around and looked at me before rolling on her back. Her lip was bruised and she looked sad. "What do you want?"

"I wanted to check on you and try to—"

"You don't believe me do you? You think I lied on your precious boyfriend."

"I wouldn't think anything like that." I said, although I did.

"Even if you don't believe me it doesn't matter. I told you and Spy I couldn't be alone and you left me anyway. And now look at what happened. I got raped again." She rolled back on her side and chuckled sarcastically before stopping suddenly. "Do me a favor, get out of my house before I go off on you. I hate bitches trying to act like they give a fuck about me."

I sat across on the other side of a glass wall, waiting on Wisdom to be brought out for our visit. It took everything in me to pull myself out of bed because since he was arrested my life turned into shit. I couldn't eat. I couldn't sleep and all of my thoughts went on my cousin, my man, my aunt. Something didn't feel right with everything but the mountain of problems was so high it was hard to see over the top.

When he finally came out he smiled, picked up the handset and sat down. He looked as bad as me. "It's not true, Carlita. You believe me right?"

"Then what happened?" I paused. "Because one minute I'm waiting on the movers with our furniture and the next you're being arrested and my cousin's face is fucked up and she's yelling rape."

"I know how it looks. I swear I do but the only thing I'm guilty of is trying to console her. Her house was burned down, she said by your aunt and she wanted to have a drink with me. The next thing I know she's jumping on me crying rape, hitting me in the back with her fists. But you know how I feel about you, Carlita." He placed his right hand over his heart. "Why would I jeopardize our relationship for that bitch?"

I frowned. "But why would she lie?"

"I don't know. If I did I wouldn't be in here or have gone anywhere near Monique. All I did was be there for her when she said she needed me. Do you think I would risk twenty years in prison for that bitch?"

I swallowed and wiped the sweat off of my brow. I didn't know what to believe. "When I went to go see her, her lip was busted. Did you do that?"

"Carlita—"

"Did you do it?" I yelled.

"Yes, but it was an accident."

Large tears began to roll down my face. If he hit her it wasn't too hard to believe that he raped her too. After all, he'd gotten forceful with me in the past. "It took a month for me to come because I wanted to be objective. I didn't want to assume the worst because I wanted us to work. Now it's clear, I can't trust you. It's over, don't call me anymore because I won't come back."

"Baby!" he yelled as he placed the palms of his hands on the glass. "Don't do this. You can't turn your back on a man like me and think it's not gonna come back to you. Please."

I looked at him once more and walked out of his life.

Forever.

CHAPTER SIXTEEN

MONIQUE

FOUR MONTHS LATER

I was on the pole, spinning and twirling at the top. I tried my best to get Poe's attention but these days he seemed frustrated. I don't know if it's me or his cousin in L.A, because he's been spending a lot of time there. At least two weekends out of the month.

When I do my next set I attempt to walk toward him, like I did when we first got together but he got up and left the front of the club. Embarrassed, I grabbed the nearest man on the floor and did the dance for him instead. When I was done I bypassed my dressing room and went toward his office.

Once there I gave myself access. "Are you okay? Because you act like you have a fucking problem with me."

"What are you talking about now?"

"I was dancing for you and you got up like I was about to shit on your lap." I walked inside and sat on the chair across from him.

"Don't sit there, Mo. I told you I don't like your bare ass on my leather chairs because my guests sit there too." He paused. "And as far as the show I'm tired of you broadcasting our relationship to my customers. I don't want no public lap dances. What we do alone is our business." He scratched his head. "What do you want?" He scanned through paperwork on his desk, without looking at me.

"I think I asked my question already, I want to know what's wrong with you. With us?"

He laughed. "What's wrong is that you have run off three girls, Monique! THREE!" He threw up three fingers like I couldn't count. "Every one of them were helping bring in customers and you got rid of them because you're jealous."

I crossed my arms over my chest and leaned against the wall. "I didn't like how they were acting. One of them stole my money even though she denied it. The other was pushing up on my clients and that white girl went to Playmates club with the other flat butt chicks so she wasn't gonna be around here long anyway."

"They left because you're rude to them. You and your fucking mother. They think just because we live together that your word is mine and that's not true. I'm trying to operate a business, Monique and I'm not about to let you run it into the ground due to jealousy."

I could tell that nothing short of apologizing would work with him so that's what I did. "I'm sorry, Poe." I walked toward him and stood at his side. "Maybe I do get a little jealous when new chicks come but it doesn't mean I'm rude or I don't love you."

"Get back over there."

I walked in front of the desk.

"It's not about love, Mo, it's about respect. You run nothing at Skeezers. I do." He looked up at me. "You're an employee like the rest. And it's high time you realize it."

I felt like I swallowed a bowling ball and no words could exit my mouth. For some reason as I stood across from him I felt like he hated me.

"Now I have a meeting with another girl in five minutes in the practice room and you can't be anywhere near the picture."

I frowned. "But I always help you select the girls."

"Not today. And not anymore." He looked me in the eyes. "Now leave, I'm busy."

I stood in front of him for one second before turning around. Once outside I fumbled toward my dressing room and grabbed an old pack of cigarettes I had in my vanity. I also grabbed my coat and walked outside. The moment I closed the door I noticed Waxton was out there too.

"What are you doing here?" I asked.

"Just did a weave on one of the girls." He looked me up and I could feel his irritation with me.

We have had money disputes in the past and although I believed we worked them out you could never tell with him. I wasn't in the mood to see him for more than one reason. "That's good."

"You got that for me yet?"

I sighed. "I'm going to give you the rest of your money, Waxton. Don't act like I'm not good for it because you know I am. Plus we already had an understanding. I was going to pay you in full on Saturday."

"I hear all that but answer me this. Did you or did you not get insurance money when your house burned down?"

"No! It's supposed to be Saturday. That's what I'm saying. They're still investigating the fire. The moment

I get the check I'll break you off, Waxton. I promise." I paused. "But look, I need you to do another favor and I'll give you five hundred more."

He crossed his arms over his chest. "What is it *this* time?"

"Poe is auditioning a new girl. Do me a favor and go check her out in the practice room. I would do it but apparently I'm not allowed inside anymore."

He rolled his eyes and sucked his teeth. "I'll do it but I want my money. I'm not fucking around with you." He left.

"I said I got you, damn!"

I smoked five stale cigarettes before Waxton came out thirty-five minutes later, which was longer than normal for any girl Poe auditioned. I mean what were they talking 'bout? He grabbed the pack of stale cigarettes and lit one. "Girl, you not gonna believe this shit."

"Believe what?"

"Who's in there dancing."

"Who is it?"

"Your cousin Spy. And when I say she burned the pole down that's exactly what I mean! She killed it!"

CHAPTER SEVENTEEN
SPYRELLA

I rushed to my silver Suburban truck where Carlita was behind the driver's seat waiting. I slid into the passenger seat and attempted to hide the grin that eased on my face. "I think I got it!" I covered my mouth with my trembling fingers. "I think he liked me!"

She laughed. "I know he likes you! Poe was always one of your biggest supporters but working in the club is another thing. You know he's picky about the girls he gets to dance! What did he say to you?"

"We talked for awhile and he asked why I wanted to dance for Skeezers. Said I was better than dancing there and at first he didn't want to see me."

Carlita frowned. "Mighty funny he didn't have no problem with me and Mo dancing."

Lately she had been snappy and jealous acting. I told myself it wasn't the case but the evidence was all in her attitude toward me. Ever since Wisdom was arrested for raping Mo and my mother for burning down her house, things had been weird in my family.

My mother claimed she didn't burn the house down but I figured it was possible since she still blamed Aunt Levine for ruining her life. To be honest I wanted my mother gone because she knew about my bulimia secret and I got the impression that if she was drunk enough she might tell him. And I would rather her be in jail and warm then on the streets and unsafe.

But this thing with Wisdom changed my favorite cousin's mood. She was always so sweet to me and now it felt like the littlest things irritated her. She was always judging me and making me feel like I didn't understand life. What she didn't get was that I was different from the Spy she knew months back. I knew a lot, like it was high time that I started doing what I wanted to do in my life.

"So how did you do?" She asked.

"Carlita." I placed my hand over my chest as I recalled the moves in my head. "I moved like a professional. I felt like I was doing ballet." I tossed my arms up. "I fucking loved it! I wished Monique was there, asked for her and everything but Poe's entire mood changed when I did. Like they having problems or something."

She smiled at me. "So you didn't see her?"

I sat back in my seat and placed on my seatbelt. "After I asked him where she was and he gave me an attitude I dropped it."

She nodded and scooped her braids over to one side of her shoulder. "Are you angry with her?"

My jaw dropped. "Angry with her? For what?"

"For everything." She positioned herself so that she could look into my eyes. "I mean why here, Spy?" she stared at the sign *Skeezers* in lights. "You could go to any club. Why does it have to be this one? A club you know Mo worships?"

"Do you miss, Mo?" I answered her question with one.

She shrugged. "Not really, I mean, I guess." She looked at the steering wheel. "Sometimes anyway. But my life has been so fucked up that lately I've been on some selfish shit. Thinking of myself."

"Well I miss her. A lot. As much as she gets on my nerves she's still my cousin and if I can be around her then I want to do that."

"And she also had aunt Diane locked up for arson too," Carlita continued. "Your mother doing ten years behind that shit."

"And my mother probably did it. To be honest I'd rather her be in jail than on the streets." I exhaled. "Back to the club, at the end of the day I always wanted to dance. Since I could remember. And now I'm doing it." I grabbed her hand. "All I'm asking is that you be happy for me."

"But what about Reggie? You don't think he'd be hurt if he found out you were here? After all, you are hiding it from him."

"Because he doesn't need to know all my moves."

She seemed annoyed with me. "Listen, I know you happy about your weight loss. You went from 300 something to 150. I get that you want attention but Reggie loves you. And he's good to you. Don't mess that up."

"I'm only doing it for a few months. Just long enough to help with the wedding expenses. With me being in school and Reggie having to pay all the bills I figured we could use the cash. I'm already tapping at my savings."

"It's your life, cuz. I'm supporting you regardless."

When we walked in the door I smelled the fried chicken Reggie was cooking and fries. He gets on my nerves with that shit. I do everything in my power to eat healthy but he stays making bad food.

"It smells good," I said as I walked up to him and kissed him. I was doing my best to hide my attitude. "What you cooking?" I already knew but wanted him to see my facial expression when he said it.

"My famous chicken." He winked at me and gave Carlita a one-arm hug. "Your cousin asked me to drop some wings a while back so I'm providing her wish."

I gave her an evil look.

"I just wanted a real meal that's all," she giggled. "I get tired of eating bird food and that stuff you be making around here, Spy. If I see one more salad I'm going to flip."

"When you moved in I thought you were gonna be on my side. You use to be on a health kick just like me."

"That's before Wisdom got locked up and I lost the house." She exhaled. "Guess it's not in me anymore to eat healthy." She looked into the frying pan and smiled halfway. "Thanks again, Reggie." She walked out of the kitchen and to her room.

"I'm sorry, baby I didn't know things were going to be that serious," he said to me. "Where you been?"

"Just grabbing some air with my cousin."

He looked down at my gym bag where my strip club clothes were hidden. "You went to the gym too?"

"Nope. I left it in the truck so I'm just taking it out now."

He removed the last wings out of the pan and placed them on the towel. As I stared at the food the only thing I thought about was how it was going to feel when I threw it back up.

"I know you didn't do it on purpose but, Reggie I don't know why you think this is cool. I'm not gonna be able to fit in my wedding dress if you keep cooking like this."

He slapped my butt. "Then we'll buy a dress that fits."

"I'm serious!"

He sighed. "Babe, I'm not gonna apologize if I like you thick. You lost half the weight you were when I met you. And I don't want you skinnier than that. So forgive me if I seduce you with food cooked out of love. Okay?"

I rolled my eyes and walked away.

Suddenly I was starting to rethink our wedding.

I was starting to rethink everything.

CHAPTER EIGHTEEN
CARLITA

I went back downstairs to eat dinner with Spy and Reggie but I felt out of place. After losing the house because I couldn't afford the mortgage and the news Wisdom was given a ten-year sentence, I preferred to spend my time doing the usual.

Crying.

If I wasn't crying I was eating. I ate so much that I gained twenty-five pounds. To make matters worse I missed Monique terribly. I wasn't being honest with Carlita because I guess I was embarrassed. Every time I tried to reach out to Mo she wouldn't accept my call.

I got the impression she didn't want to hear from me again so I was trying to give her space. But months have passed and I was hoping that things were different and that she would at least give me a chance to talk. To apologize for what Wisdom did to her.

I decided to call Skeezers since the chances of her hanging up on me would be lower. But when I called I got Waxton instead. He didn't work there so it was weird. "Who the fuck is this?" He yelled at me.

I laughed and stopped when I realized he was answering the phone at a place of business. "Waxton, are you okay? This is Carlita. And why you answering the phone at the club?"

Now he laughed. "I'm answering the phone because your cousin is a bitch and she threw my cell phone when I told her I had some T recorded on her. Yeah, the bitch didn't know I had that."

"I don't know what's going on but you better mind your tongue with talking about my cousin like that."

"Bitch, I'll say whatever I want. Now what do you need because I'm leaving."

I heard some bottles rattling in the background. "What is all that noise?"

"Well let me tell you. First off that cousin of yours is not a woman of her word. I'm so sick of that bitch stiffing me for her weaves and the little jobs I do around here. I don't know what made you leave that house but you did good because the whore is crazy."

I sat on the edge of my bed because it seemed like he knew more than he was telling me. "You talk a lot of shit for a nigga who stay up her ass. I thought ya'll were so close."

"Chile, I may have been close to her but she wasn't hardly close to me. And she wasn't close to you either. Now I know this if fucked up but while I'm raiding this bar to collect what's owed to me, let me put you on to a few things. First off Monique paid me to burn down her house so she could be up in Poe's bed. And she also paid me to get her the Rufi's she used to set Wisdom up for rape."

I swallowed the lump in my throat and sat up. "Waxton, you're scaring me...I...I don't understand. Are you saying that all of this, everything that I've been going through over the past few months was a lie?"

"I'm telling you that your cousin is pure evil. And I'm telling you that you need to stay wherever you are because she is the worst kind." He started laughing. "Had she not broken my phone I would've emailed you the proof to get Wisdom out of jail but thank your cousin for that shit. I recorded her offering to pay me for the drugs, the arson and everything."

"So you're saying that he never, never touched her?"

"I ain't say all that shit." He laughed. "Don't know if your cousin and man told you but they fucked before. I think Mo's grimy ass was mad because she wanted more and he wasn't feeling her."

"Waxton, I really hope you're not lying to me."

"Lie to you for what, darling? I'm grown." He exhaled. "Now I've said enough. I have to go. Good luck with your situation. I points out the mess but I don't cleans 'em." He hung up.

I can't remember the last time I was this angry. As a matter of fact I don't remember ever being this angry in my life. And yet here I was, standing in the middle of my bedroom thinking the vilest thoughts imaginable. Learning that Monique broke my heart this way made me think of doing the most horrific things.

But I had to be easy. I had to be smart, after all everything she does is calculating. I want her put away but not by telling the police. Not yet anyway.

I wanted her ruined.

When I walked back toward Monique's dressing room I could hear her yelling and calling Waxton a gay bitch.

And since the bar was completely empty I figured she was talking to him on the phone because he was obviously gone. When I made it to her room she was walking in circles screaming. Her hair was in a cornrowed beehive which meant she was supposed to get a weave. "Fuck you then, you hoe ass bitch! And just for that I'm not paying you shit!" She tossed her phone on the dresser.

I stood in her doorway and tried my best to appear humble. Or, like she liked her friends, naive. "Is everything okay, cousin?"

She looked at me and rolled her eyes. "What the fuck you doing here?" She flopped in the chair.

"I wanted to talk to you, Monique. I can tell you upset so I'm gonna make it quick."

She rolled her eyes again. "Please do."

"I can't believe after all of this time we still aren't speaking." I walked deeper into her dressing room. "I know you don't believe this but after what Wisdom did to you I realized you were always right about him. The fucked up part was you shouldn't have gotten hurt for me to realize it."

She crossed her arms over her chest. "You know how to do weave right?"

Fuck is this bitch talking about?

"Not as good as Waxton but I'm okay. Remember, I use to do them for you when you were in between appointments and he was booked up."

She reached under the table, threw a bag of hair on top of it and looked at me. "Since you're so apologetic come over here and do my shit."

I placed my purse on the chair and walked over to her. Taking the hair out of the bag I used the scissors to cut the weave, and then funneled five needles with black thread, placing them on the dresser. When I was ready I walked over to her and said, "So what happened with Waxton? Why you so mad at him?"

"No reason." She shrugged, guilt painted all over her face.

"All that or no reason? You sounded like you were going through the roof."

She sighed. "He's not the friend I thought he was, let's put it that way." She waved the air. "Anyway I need your help with something. Something very important."

"What's that?"

"Have you spoken to Spy?"

"Sometimes," I lied. She didn't need to know that we lived together. "Why?"

"Because she has the nerve to be dancing here. Apparently she lost weight and wants to throw her pussy around my mothafuckin' club. You and me both know how she feels about Poe so I need her gone. But I don't have a plan."

I exhaled. "I'm not gonna lie, I love Spy because she's my cousin too. But I will never choose her over you. Give me a few days and watch, I'll come up with the ultimate plan."

CHAPTER NINETEEN

SPYRELLA

Tonight was the night and I almost didn't make it. I tried to talk myself out of it so many times I was almost late for my set. But as I looked through the mirror, at Poe who was standing behind me, staring, giving me that look that made my pussy moist, well…let's just say that I'm glad I came.

When his mouth moved I realized I couldn't hear him. At first I didn't understand why. And then I remembered. When I was around him time stopped. Everything was silent. It took a moment to realize I was in the packed dressing room, full of women scantily clothed and wearing too much perfume. Unlike my cousin, who I haven't seen yet, I didn't have a private space.

"Okay everybody out!" Poe yelled to the girls. "It's time to work the floors." He clapped his hands loudly.

They excitedly put the finishing touches on their outfits and quickly exited. There were big drug dealers in the building so the payout today was going to be huge at the bar and for the dancers.

When we were alone I thought about what I was doing again by being here. Who was I fooling? I may have dabbled in dancing a little back in the day but stripping? I was finally realizing I was out of my league. "I don't want to go out there." I looked up at him. "I think I'm making a mistake."

"Then don't go. You don't have to do this, Spy." He was calm and sincere which was refreshing.

"But I thought about doing this for so long. If I leave…"

He sat next to me. "This life…where you dance for men who want your attention is temporary. You can't do this forever. I can't even do this shit forever and I'm behind the scenes."

I looked away because he was difficult to stare at without thinking unclean stuff. "I thought you loved this. The club. The money. The lights."

"I love setting out to do something and doing that. Plus my father left me this spot so I wanted to make it work. But to tell you the truth I could leave it in an instant. Especially if I had a reason."

I looked down at my hands. "She hates me you know? I knocked on her door when I got here and she wouldn't open it."

He exhaled, his mood now stiff. "She'll be alright. I had to put out five thousand dollars in liquor because that faggy mothafucka she rolls with robbed me. I told her she couldn't dance tonight and Mo's use to getting what she wants. It ain't happening this time."

"I'm surprised to hear your relationship is changed. I always thought you two looked good together."

He stood up and I felt I said something wrong. "Spy, why here? Why this club?" He paused. "Is it to get at Mo? For all the bad things she said to you? Because if that's the reason you should leave. It's the wrong way."

"No...I dreamed of dancing here. I remember when Carlita and Mo use to come home, sometimes with large coats hiding their dancing outfits, I thought they were glamorous. And I wanted the same thing for me." I exhaled. "But now that I'm here, I feel there's another reason I'm drawn to this club." I looked at him and then away.

What am I doing?

"Spy, with the talent you have it doesn't have to be wasted in this place. If you want to be here I support that but I want you to know where I'm coming from too. If at anytime you decide to leave, I'll hold your hand and help you down."

I danced off three songs and there was more money falling out of the sky than I knew what to do with. With all of the attention I was receiving I felt on top of the world, and at the same time, a feeling I wasn't willing to acknowledge existed.

What if Poe was right? What if I wasn't supposed to be living like this?

When I looked across the room I noticed him staring at me. And when I gave him eye contact he looked away. He did that often. I knew it was wrong to be playing the eye game with him but it didn't stop me from thinking about our life if he gave girls like me chances.

I was finished my set and was about to get off the stage so Ohio, a white girl with pretty good butt injections, could dance. But everyone was calling for me to stay and when I looked at Poe he nodded with approval. Turning around to Ohio I said, "My bad, they want me to—"

"Do what you gotta!" She threw her hand up and stormed off.

I shrugged, and stayed on the stage until every wallet was empty.

When I walked outside of the club Carlita was waiting in the truck. She unlocked the door and I slid into the passenger seat. She was smiling widely and didn't seem as dark as she had in the past. "Well…how did it go, cousin? And don't leave out one detail!"

I thought about my night and opened my purse, revealing a stash of cash. It was so full I could barely close it. "With the money I made tonight I think I'm done. It's more than enough to help Reggie with the wedding."

She frowned. "Done?" Her expression was heavy with disappointment. "Why you say that?"

"All I wanted was to see if I could do it and collect a little cash. I'm done now." I sighed. "Plus if I stay, I think I'll get into another kind of trouble." Poe's face flashed in my mind.

She shook her head as if she disapproved. "Spy, at first I wasn't for this but now I see how excited you are. Maybe you should hang in there a little longer. Have some fun."

"It's worse than that, Carlita." I thought about Poe and my developing feelings for him. "I don't want to disrespect Reggie. I don't want to disrespect our wedding more than I have already. Plus what if one of his friends walks in and sees me."

She waved me off. "Girl, me and you both know that boy ain't got no friends." She paused. "I think you should stay for a few more months until you get it out of your system. This is your time to shine and Reggie is gonna have to understand."

I looked out of the window at the Skeezers sign. "Are you sure?"

"I'm positive."

I sighed. "Well even if I do stay I'll get my cycle in a few days. I won't be able to dance anyway."

"If you don't bleed heavy all you gotta do is cut the string off the tampon. You'll be fine." She exhaled. "Anyway before we leave I have to use the bathroom. But think about what I said. You didn't come this far to dance one night. Have a little fun and I'll tell you when it's time to stop. Don't worry, you can trust me."

CHAPTER TWENTY

CARLITA

After I used the bathroom, which I forced myself to do since I didn't really have to go, I made sure to run into Poe. "Oh hey, how you been?" I asked hugging him as he gripped me back. "I don't know why I didn't think you were here tonight."

"Where else would I be?" he joked. He released me.

"In L.A., heard you been spending a lot of time there."

"Yeah, I'm back and forth a lot." He nodded. He seemed heavier than he was before he got with Mo and I knew she was driving him insane. "You taking care of yourself?"

"I'm good, considering everything I had going on." I thought about Wisdom and my heart ached. It didn't make things better after realizing that everything that happened was Mo's fault.

"Yeah, I still can't wrap my mind around the shit with Wisdom either. I fucked with dude."

I shrugged. "Me too but maybe he wasn't for me."

He looked into my eyes. "So you believe he did it?"

I nodded yes. "Why, don't you?"

He cleared his throat. "So what brought you here?"

"I'm taking Spy home, she's out in the truck." She smiled. "I don't know what you're doing in here but you have her on cloud nine."

He smiled but wiped it away. "That girl not thinking about me."

I looked into his eyes and saw something I didn't see before. He liked her. He probably always had but nobody could see it because of Spy's body shape. Who could see someone as fine as him with her? "I wasn't going to tell you this but she has something for you."

His head leaned toward me and he pointed to himself. "What you talking about? She hardly ever said two words to me. Not even when we were in high school when I asked her to the prom."

My jaw dropped because I remembered that day but my recollection was from another point of view. "Wait, you asked Spy first or Mo first?"

He chuckled. "I always, always, looked at Mo as a friend. I love her I can't lie but back then it was never like that between us. When I decided to go to the prom I wanted to go with Spy but she shot me down."

I was trying to hide the shock but it was heavy. If Spy had one clue that this man wanted her I'm certain she would not have been with Reggie. "I don't think she knows that you wanted her to go to the prom."

"Why? I asked her."

"Right after you asked I remember Mo telling her that you only asked due to charity. Because you felt bad for her or some shit like that."

"But Spy wasn't even big back then. She was as beautiful back in the day as she was when she gained the weight." He scratched his head. "This shit fucks me up. Don't know why that girl gotta be so evil."

"I'm just telling you what Mo told Spy," I said.

He laughed but I could tell he was angry. "That's Mo for you."

"Exactly, the sad part is Spy has a thing for you. If only you weren't with Mo things could've been different."

"Wait, she told you that?"

"Yep." I looked dead into his eyes. "Just now but she doesn't want you to know. So you have to keep that between us."

He seemed frustrated. He ran his hand down his face and sighed. "Look, I have to get back home, plus

Mo's here somewhere lurking. She was off today and came by to get something out her dressing room. That was five hours ago." He walked closer. "But do me a favor, keep this info between us. I don't want to have a conversation with Mo about this later."

"You can trust me."

He kissed me on the cheek and walked away. And since my plan to destroy Mo was coming together better than I could have imagined, I decided to go into her dressing room and fuck with her a little bit. When I walked inside she was standing up, angrily stuffing some hair products in her black Celine bag. "Are you okay?" I asked.

She turned around and walked toward me. "Any ideas yet? On getting rid of that bitch?"

"What bitch?" I wanted to play games although I knew exactly what she meant.

"Spy's ass! I heard she made more money than me tonight! And since it's obviously some fluke shit I don't want her thinking she can do this type thing every night."

"You know she's out front of the club, waiting on me right?"

She rolled her eyes and walked away. "I thought you hadn't spoken to her."

"That was before you told me you wanted me to get her out of here. I moved in with her and everything to make sure the plan is perfect."

"I don't know about this."

"Mo you gonna have to let me play this shit out. You can't control everything like you're use to. If you want my help I need you to back up."

"I will."

"I'm serious!"

"As desperate as I am to get that bitch gone I'm willing to do anything."

CHAPTER TWENTY-ONE
CARLITA

I was sitting next to Poe in Skeezers, watching Spy dance. I had my own plan in play but I couldn't get over how good she was. I knew she could dance but after the weight I'm not gonna lie, I didn't think she had it anymore.

She proved me wrong.

When I looked over I saw Poe staring her down and I leaned over to him. "She's great isn't she?"

He cleared his throat, pulled out his cell phone and pretended to be texting someone. "She's good…not bad at all. She was worried at first but she's a natural."

I laughed. "I can't believe you're acting like I don't know the truth. If anything you can trust me, we grew up together."

"I can't think about anything like that right now, Carlita." He put his phone on the table. "Me and Mo had another fight and tonight I'm gonna tell her she has to leave my crib. And the club." He exhaled. "I know it's fucked up but I can't deal with her anymore.

We keep what we got going on and I may start hating her."

I tried to hide the excitement in my face but it was hard. Mo had gotten Poe so fucked up that he was doing my dirty work. I had plans to destroy their relationship personally but he beat me to the punch. "Oh, Poe, I'm so sorry. Is there anything I can do?"

"Not for me but you may want to be there for your cousin."

I tried to fake compassion for Mo but it was hard and I'm sure was coming across dishonestly. "I'll try but we haven't been the same since Wisdom and the rape. Truthfully I'm more concerned with your happiness." I looked at the stage at Spy. "And hers." I paused. "Because she's really feeling you."

He wiped his hand down his face. "This shit is crazy, Carlita. I don't like doing things like this. At all."

"You know she wants you. Me and Spy talked about it." I lied. "The only thing is she's getting married next month, Poe so if you want to at least tell her how you feel now is the time."

He looked at the stage again but Spy was gone already and Ohio was dancing in her place. "I don't know about getting too serious but I do want to clear up the stuff you were telling me about prom night. We were kids but still. I want her to know the truth."

"So what are you waiting on? Tell her!"

"When?"

"Tonight…and I can set the whole thing up."

We were on our third drink at Christian's Steakhouse in Washington DC. I was having so much fun that I almost forgot that the plan was to drive nails into Mo's coffin. We had eaten dinner, dessert and poured drink after drink down our throats. Through it all Spy and Poe laughed at one another's jokes and touched each other softly while making points. Everything looked innocent but it was anything but.

Cheating and betrayal was in the air.

Since Christian's was also a lounge, they were playing soft R&B music and I knew it was just a matter of time for them to play the song I paid for. A song I knew Poe couldn't resist, *"How Can I Love U 2nite"*. The moment the song came on his eyes widened and I tried to look surprised. Like I hadn't set the shit up and kept pressing the DJ out to play it every five minutes. "Hold up, you still love this song Poe?"

He blushed and tried to hide his smile. "Yeah, its alright."

"Well what are you waiting on?" I nudged him. "Dance with Spy."

"No, we can't do that," Spy interjected. "It would be too weird. He's my boss."

"I'm not your boss," Poe said seriously. "I'll fire you before you look at me in that way."

Wow. He didn't want anything fucking up this night.

"Look, we out having drinks and I know ya'll both like the song. Hurry up before it goes off." When they didn't move I was getting frustrated. "Stop tripping. This is a no strings attached type of night. Enjoy it."

"She's right." Finally he got up and extended his hand. When she rose too I wanted to explode.

Now the next part of my plan was about to take off. I waited for two verses of the song to play and quickly moved toward them. "Poe, I want another drink and the man says I need your credit card since the waiters are changed. Something about needing to close out the first bill."

My statement was dumb but he reached in his pocket and I hoped my plan would work. Instead of handing me the card he gave me his wallet. I smiled, walked away and went to the counter. Out of Poe's view I went through his wallet, looking for that one thing. And when I found it I tried to hide my grin again.

With the safety pin I eased out of my purse in my palm, I poked a whole through the condom wrapper. When I was done I placed it back and waited for them to come back. Since Spy's period passed about two weeks ago I figured she was ovulating and hoped it was now.

"Have fun?" I asked them. I handed Poe back his wallet and he stuffed it in his pocket without altercation.

Spy was grinning widely while Poe was trying to appear calm. "It was nice," she said. She looked at him. "Really nice."

"Well that's good. Unfortunately I forgot I have something to do tonight so I'm going to take your truck and leave."

"Wait, how am I going to get home?" she asked.

"Reggie is out of town, let Poe take you."

She looked scared. "I don't know about this, Carlita. I'm already—"

"Spy, I wish you would relax! There's absolutely nothing to worry about. All you're doing is hanging out with an old friend. A friend you've known longer than Reggie. Nothing more nothing less. And what you gonna do, go home and watch Netflix with me all night? It's stupid."

She looked at me and then at him. "Well...I guess it's okay." She shrugged. "If Poe don't mind dropping me off I'll see you later."

I got up and ran out before either of them changed their minds.

CHAPTER TWENTY-TWO
SPYRELLA

I can't believe I'm sitting in the front area of an Embassy Suites hotel room. I can't believe I was sitting with him but at the same time being with him felt so right. "You were always a bully," I said to him as I held another glass of Hennessy with coke in my hand.

He pointed at himself. "Me…a bully? Since when did I bully anybody?"

"When we were in school anything you wanted to do we did. Now I'm not gonna lie, you had good taste so I didn't mind but still."

"Man, I just wanted everybody to have a good time," he laughed. "Plus when I asked ya'll what the plan was nobody ever said anything. It was crazy being the only dude in our group."

There was silence between us for a minute before I remembered Reggie, and my upcoming wedding. "I don't know what this is, between us. I feel like I'm going down a street I've never been to before."

"We're just chilling, Spy. Like I said in the restaurant I always wanted to spend time with you. And even though you're beautiful now I thought you were pretty before you lost weight." He looked at my body but not in a way that made me uncomfortable. "What did you do?"

"Threw up," I joked. Maybe it was the liquor or maybe I wanted to admit that I had bulimia to someone. It just so happened to be a man I cared about more than I wanted to admit.

"You joking right?"

I hung my head down but remained silent.

He moved closer and placed his hand over mine. "Spy, you gotta be kidding me. Why would you hurt yourself like that?"

I was about to get him together because the last thing I needed was someone judging me. It's bad enough that Reggie did all he could to sabotage my diet, so that I wouldn't eat good food and now this. What I wanted to do with my body was my business and I was tired of making excuses. I had a lot of shit to tell him but the moment I opened my mouth I started crying instead.

I knew he was right about hurting myself but I was so deep into my process to lose weight that I didn't know how I was going to stop. One moment I was living with Mo and Carlita being a fat housekeeper and the next I was dancing on the pole, my body better than it had been in my life.

How could I stop something that had proven to work?

As I continued to cry he held me not saying a word and I appreciated him for it. It took me about an hour to calm down before he finally spoke. "Spy, I'm not judging you. And I don't know what you were going through to make you feel hurting yourself was the only way. But I can help you if you want. I can work with you to stay fit but please, please…not like this."

He said the most perfect words. And for some reason I found myself in his arms. Although we were in the living room portion of the hotel we were on the floor. A few hugs and pulls and before long I was naked, his warm body on top of mine.

After putting on his condom he moved into my pussy and it was slow and passionate. At that moment I could tell that he liked me the entire time because he looked at me the same way he did whenever he would show up at the house. I just wouldn't allow myself to see it.

For a moment I wondered what my life would be like if we were together. It was useless. Our time with each other was for the moment and tomorrow he would be back with Mo and me with Reggie.

I had to be realistic, to keep things in perspective.

But why did it hurt so bad?

I couldn't believe I overslept. Even though Reggie was out of town I knew he was coming home later that day, I just hoped it wasn't before I got home.

Since I was late Poe and I decided that it was best to put me in an Uber. A mile away from my house I couldn't stop playing my time with Poe over in my mind. He was so kind and sweet and I felt at home in his arms. Reggie never cared enough to hold me after sex so when we were done it was almost like I was alone. He'd fall into a bear like snore and wouldn't so much as touch me.

I thought the night was special until he grabbed me and looked into my eyes before I left. "Make sure he's the man for you. I'm not saying it's me because we never had the chance to get to know one another. I never had the chance to fight for you because I was afraid of how miserable Monique would make your life. But I'm asking you to be sure you want to be with him forever before you say yes."

I was so confused I didn't know what to do. Mainly because he was right.

When the Uber dropped me off my heart almost jumped out of my chest when I saw Reggie's car in the front of the house. I didn't have a firm time on when he would be back but I hoped he would text me. Seeing his Escalade next to Carlita's Honda had my mind spinning. But where was my truck?

I got out the car, took a deep breath and walked inside the house, hoping a lie would come to me when I got inside. I also hoped Carlita would know where my truck was. The moment I opened the door Carlita was standing in front of me. In a deep whisper she said, "He's in the shower and I told him you went to the grocery store to get some things for breakfast. I parked your truck around the corner." She stuffed my keys into my hand. "Put 'em in your pocket."

"I knew I heard the front door. Where you been?" Reggie asked walking down the steps with a red towel wrapped around his body. "I thought you went to the store."

"I didn't give her the money," Carlita said answering for me. "So she came back." She had a roll of bills in the other hand and she handed them to me. She was awfully prepared.

Although I appreciated her speaking up, I mean *really appreciated* her, I felt like something was going on. There was darkness behind her eyes I hadn't always seen.

Reggie looked at me and I wasn't sure if he believed her or not. "Naw, I got it." He walked to the kitchen, grabbed his wallet off the counter and opened it. He gave me one hundred bucks and gave Carlita's money back. "I missed you, baby." He placed his huge hands on the side of my face. "You know that right?" He moved his hands to my shoulders where he massaged them roughly.

"Yeah…I…of course."

"I would do anything for you, Spy. *Anything*." His stare was intense and I knew he sensed I wasn't faithful. He didn't trust me and since I just finished sucking Poe's dick I knew why.

"I know, Reggie. I love you."

He winked. "I'm going upstairs. Get me some grits and bacon. I'm starved." He walked away.

I took a deep breath and Carlita rushed up to me. She looked behind her to make sure he was gone and then stared at me again. "Are you okay?"

"I gotta leave that nigga alone. I can't see him again," I whispered.

"By nigga you mean Poe?" she asked in a low voice.

"You know who I mean, Carlita. I feel like you set all of this up too. Me, Poe, the hotel all of this shit."

At first she was looking confused and then a look of confirmation came over her face. "You're right. This is my doing."

I was shocked. "Why?"

"I set it up because you deserve to be with the man you want and if you think its Reggie you're in for a ruined life." She looked at me and walked away.

CHAPTER TWENTY-THREE

MONIQUE

"I don't understand what I've done, Poe. I know we've had problems but this is too far. You're not even trying to make it work." I sat on the sofa in our house and he was next to me stiff and unemotional.

Normally if I cried he would be there to wipe my tears. He once told me he could deal with a stranger spitting on him more than he could a crying woman. I guess that was then and this is now. He'd been cold for the past few months but today he was vicious. Like he didn't care or know me.

He touched my hand and I pulled it away. "I don't mean to hurt you, Mo. But I can't live like this anymore."

"You say you don't want this but you're hurting my feelings anyway! Can't we go back to our friendship? Before we had sex?"

"Shit is fucked up though and we can't even be friends right now. This is why I begged you to think about it before we went there. I knew something like this could happen and now look."

"But you're the only man I ever loved, Poe. I gave up everything and everybody to be with you."

"And I never asked you." He stood up and walked toward the breakfast window by the kitchen. "I'm not happy." He placed his hand on his chest. "I haven't been for a long time and I need that to stop."

"Who is it?" I crossed my arms over my chest. "Just tell me straight up since you keeping shit so real now."

"You not even listening. That's why we can't work because you never hear what I'm saying. You put in your mind what you want and you run with it, even if it's a lie."

"You just met her didn't you?" My vision was blurred because I was crying so hard and I felt myself wanting to hurt him. Not only for breaking my heart, but also for not wanting me.

"I want you out of my house, Mo. And because I know you got to get on your feet I'll give you keys to my apartment out Bmore. It's fully furnished so you don't have to worry about anything. You'll be comfortable there for awhile."

"So you're coming too? Because that's the only way I'll be comfortable, Poe."

"You have to leave."

He was firm and his statement sounded final. "So you kicking me out the club too?"

"We can't live or work together. It all ends here." He grabbed his keys off the counter and stuffed them in his pocket. When he left I dropped to my knees and screamed.

Carlita was over Poe's house with me, helping me pack my things. I didn't have furniture so I was only taking my clothes. Poe came back about an hour earlier and dropped off $5,000, his attempt to make up for ruining my life with cash. But it wasn't about the money. With the cash I made from dancing I saved up over $60,000.

What I really wanted was him.

"I know something else is going on." I looked over at her. "We've had our problems but it's someone else."

Carlita walked over to me and sat down. "I'm so sorry, Monique. I wanted you to get everything you deserved but this…" she looked around. "This is so cold."

I wiped my tears with the back of my hand. "I know, it's too much. Now I wished we never fucked because at least he would still love me."

She placed a warm hand on my leg. "I know, I know but you can handle it. As a matter of fact I'm surprised you're crying, seeing as how heartless you are and all."

I looked at her and tilted my head. "What you talking about?"

She laughed hysterically. "You don't think I know the truth? You didn't think it would find me and that I would call you out on all of your shit?" Huh? Did you really think you were invincible?"

"Carlita, I don't know what you talking about but I don't have time for this shit right now."

"You will have time for it, bitch!" she yelled. "You better be lucky I'm not a killer because you'd be dead. Outside of Poe breaking your heart which is priceless. The only thing better than this is death."

My heart rocked in my chest because I knew she was talking about Wisdom. How did she know I set him up on the rape charge? I didn't tell anybody but...anybody but...Waxton. "I know you better get out of my face before I smack the shit out of you."

I wanted this girl out of this house so I could figure everything out.

Did Poe know?

"I'm gonna get out of your face when I get ready." She pointed her finger in my face. "Just understand I was half the reason you lost the nigga of your dreams. Although you had more to do with it with your selfish attitude."

"What are you talking about, Carlita?"

"I'm talking about I facilitated Spy and Poe getting together. And if I did my job she will be pregnant and married within the year. The hilarious part is this, who would've thought that they would be an item?" He paused. "Or maybe you knew the entire time which is why you wanted her out of that club. And treated her so badly in front of him."

I jumped up. "You don't know what the fuck you talking about! He would never choose her over me."

"He has, bitch. And you deserve all of it!" she was screaming and she looked like a rapid dog. "I fucking loved you! And what did you do? You took away my life just because I moved out of the house! So tell me something, is it true that you fucked Wisdom?"

"Leave!"

"Is it fucking true?"

I swallowed. "Whatever we did it was before ya'll got together."

I walked to my door because I needed to think and the way she was acting I didn't feel safe. I had my shit with me but I loved Poe with all my heart. "Just go, Carlita!"

She walked toward the door with a smirk on her face. "You will be lonely for the rest of your life. And I want you to remember my face and know that your misery was because of me!"

"And I wish you all the misery back! Everything you wish for me you will have yourself! I promise!" I slammed the door in her face.

CHAPTER TWENTY-FOUR
CARLITA

I kept replaying the look in her eyes repeatedly in my mind. Although my plan to ruin her life won't stop until she's locked up for burning down her own house, blaming our aunt and lying on Wisdom, I was satisfied so far with the way things were going.

I told Poe earlier that I wanted to meet with him later, to tell him some of the things that were on my heart. The plan was to give him all the details about the fire and encourage him to file charges. I wasn't sure if I could get Wisdom out of jail if my plan worked but I was realizing it didn't matter. Time had shown me that maybe I didn't need him. Maybe I didn't need anybody for anything. I was growing self-sufficient.

After waiting five minutes my aunt Diane finally came out to visit me. Although she was wearing orange she looked better than she did since the last time I saw her. At peace. I was excited to give her the news that could set her free.

I gave her a hug and she sat across the table from me. She gazed behind me. "Where's Spy?"

"She's not here, Auntie. I kind of wanted to talk to you alone."

She looked disappointed. Clearing her throat she nodded and said, "Okay, what's going on?"

"I found out that Monique lied on you. Set you up for burning her house. Now I know who's involved and he may fight me at first but I think we can convince him to—"

"Leave it alone, Carlita. Let it go."

I sat back and looked at her like she was crazy. "Did you hear what I said?" I was so excited I couldn't contain myself. "If we work together we can get you out of prison!"

She frowned at me. "What happened to you? I see hate all over you and that was never your thang. You were always so sweet, Carlita. Have you allowed Monique to change you? If you have I beg you to slow down and get your life together." She paused. "If you don't you'll regret it."

I laughed. "I always knew you were weak but I was hoping that now you would want to fight. Especially since someone put you in prison for something you didn't do. Now I find out you like being here."

"I didn't burn down Mo's house but I burned down many. And you know what, I'm tired of being angry and I'm tired of running. All I want is peace and if I can get it after spending ten years in prison than so be it."

I stood up, looked down at her and frowned. "I always thought you were weird, living outside and all. Now I realize you're also a push over. If you want to die in here instead of fighting that bitch for your freedom than keel over." I spit in her face, and walked out.

When I opened the door to Spy's house I was shocked to see Reggie standing next to the table with the house phone dangling in his hand. His face looked red and it looked like he'd been crying. When I walked further inside he slammed the phone down and stormed over to me. "Is it true?"

I raised my eyebrows, confused. With a smile I said, "Reggie, what's wrong? You and Spy fighting again?"

"Is it true!" He yelled so loud my eardrums rocked.

It took me time to compute everything in my mind but I was finally getting it. He had spoken to Monique. I didn't understand how it was possible until I remembered I told her I lived with Spy and I called her a few times from this number. *Stupid!* That mistake was going to cost Spy.

Oh well.

Even if it did it didn't much matter because Spy was going to get the man of her dreams. In the end I was doing her a favor and she should thank me. When it came to choosing between Poe and Reggie, Reggie didn't have a chance. "I'm not sure what you're talking about." I placed my purse on the counter, walked to the refrigerator and opened it.

He slammed it shut and when I looked down at his hand I saw a gun. My heart rocked and I could barely breathe. "Reggie, what are you doing?" I raised my hands and backed away from him but the stove prevented me from going any further.

"Did Spy cheat on me with some nigga who owns a strip club?"

My mind twirled. Should I tell him the truth? And if I did would he blame me? The problem was I didn't know how much Monique said and what she didn't. "I think you're confused because you know that Spy—"

"DID SHE FUCK SOME NIGGA WHO OWN A STRIP CLUB OR NOT?" Spit flew from his mouth as he yelled in my face.

I nodded yes. I didn't want Spy having to deal with his anger but right now he was in my face with a gun. It was me or her and I wanted to live.

"You have no idea how much she fucked up with me. I had many women! Women who would've done anything I asked and I get treated like this from a bitch who throws up to be thin!"

I remained silent, afraid to move or say the wrong thing.

He pointed the gun in my face and I jumped. My belly rumbled. "Reggie, please, please don't hurt me."

He lowered the gun. "Whatever happens next is your fault."

After he left I rushed to the phone. I had to call Spy and Poe because I was afraid where Reggie would go next. If he caught them together only God knows what would happen. I called Spy five times and she didn't answer. Then I called Poe a few times and the same thing. On a hunch I decided to call Skeezers because I knew a tech was scheduled to clean the ventilation system.

About thirty minutes later I dialed the number and the first voice I heard caused my blood to run cold. It was my aunt Levine. "CARLITA, SHE'S DEAD! MY BABY'S DEAD!"

"Auntie, I don't...understand..."

"Monique is dead!"

When I got to Skeezers I parked sideways and jumped out. There were police cars everywhere and a few fire trucks. It looked like a scene out of a horror movie, except it wasn't.

It was obvious. Reggie got here and made good on his promise that whatever happened next would be my fault.

But why kill Monique?

The answer to all of my questions came to a sudden stop when I saw the face of the man I once loved. He was thrown in handcuffs and pushed in back of a police car.

What was Wisdom doing here?

Confused I ran into the club, disregarding several police officers who told me to stop. When I saw my aunt talking to a detective I ran up to her and hugged her tightly. Interrupting the investigation I said, "Aunt Levine, what happened?"

"Ma'am, this is an investigation," the officer said to me. He was stern and rude.

"Please, one second, sir." My body trembled and I thought I would erupt. "This is my family and I have to know what's going on."

"It was Wisdom!" Aunt Levine said pushing past the investigator. "Monique was here to get the rest of her things when..." She cried harder.

"But Wisdom was locked up!" Tears were rolling down my eyes and I found it hard to see. I wanted Monique to get killed, even wished for it. And now that it happened I felt gut punched.

Like my world had ended.

"He's been out for a week," the officer said. "Free on a technicality in his case. He may have been plotting and waiting this whole time and nobody knew he was home." he paused. "How did you know him?"

"He was my fiancé. Before he was arrested." I wiped the tears away. "Auntie, I don't understand! It's before business hours! Who let him in?"

"When we got here to let the technicians in he…he was already here!" I figured he must've kept his key to the club from when he use to be a bartender. "He walked up to her and said…and said, 'This is for lying'. And he pulled the trigger!"

CHAPTER TWENTY-FIVE
CARLITA

I decided I had to get to Poe's house but the problem was it had been so long that I forgot where he lived. It took me two hours to find the right street and in between that time I had called both of them a million times.

Why weren't they answering the phone?

I was afraid Monique told him where Poe lived and he would come for them.

When I finally found the brick house, located on a tree-lined street, I parked in front of a fire hydrant and rushed toward his door. I was about to knock until I looked in Poe's truck and saw them sitting inside. I ran up to it and banged on the windows heavily. They both jumped but relaxed when they recognized me.

Poe unlocked the door and I slipped inside the backseat. "Why don't ya'll have your fucking phones?" I yelled. "I've been calling you for hours!" When I noticed their melancholy mood didn't match mine I knew something was up. "What's wrong?"

Spy wiped the tears from her eyes. "I can't be with Reggie and I don't know how to tell him. We been trying to work it out."

"But where are your phones?" I repeated after hearing their situation was nowhere near as dramatic as mine.

"Mine is on the charger inside," Poe said.

"And I left mine in my purse, in the bedroom. We were going to get something to eat right quick and the conversation got deep." Spy looked at me. "But what's wrong? You're scaring me."

"It's Monique, she's been killed."

"What the fuck?" Poe yelled while Spy broke down crying, screaming so loudly I could hardly hear him. "What do you mean?"

It wasn't until that moment that I started sobbing too. Everything was happening so quickly that I didn't get a chance to process. I finally understood what happened. My cousin was murdered and I was responsible for the next load of drama coming their way.

I told them how Wisdom was released early and killed her for lying on him about the rape. There was so much pain in the car over Mo's death that I forgot about the point for me being there.

Reggie was on the loose.

"There's something else," I said softly. My temples throbbed. "Before Monique was killed she told Reggie about you two. And I think he'll be—" Suddenly there was a burning sensation on my arm and I witnessed glass shattering everywhere.

When I looked to my right I saw Reggie's open truck door but where was he? I got my answer when the front windshield shattered. He was standing in front of the car unloading bullets into the vehicle. For some reason I couldn't hear anything, maybe this was all a nightmare, one that I would wake up from soon.

CHAPTER TWENTY-SIX

SEVEN MONTHS LATER

The sun shined down on a beautiful home in Marina del Ray in California. Nine month pregnant Spy was making coffee while Poe sat at the kitchen table, looking at the new menus. Spy got help with her bulimia and she focused all her efforts on a healthy pregnancy. The doctors weren't optimistic. If she wanted her child she had to fight because one of the long-term issues with bulimia is infertility.

Life for them was special but there was always the air of the many who died in their quest to be with each other. Although they took the blame for Reggie, who was gunned down by the police after a high-speed chase shootout on the beltway, they didn't feel responsible for Mo's death. Especially after learning about her lies against Wisdom who had been given twenty-five to life for murder.

Although they had each other, Poe and Spy didn't go unharmed.

Poe suffered two gunshots, one in his chest and the other in his leg. Spy was shot in her thigh and they both quickly recovered.

It was Carlita who suffered the most.

After the coffee was made Spy poured her new husband a cup and kissed him on the lips. He rubbed her belly and said, "I love you."

"I know." She kissed him again.

"How is she today?"

"Not good. Still has her moments but I'm trying to keep her spirits up."

He nodded. "Well I have a meeting with my cousin for the new restaurant later. If you want me to come back early so you can get some air I can do that. I don't want you stressed while you carrying my baby."

She touched her belly. "I'll be fine, really. But if you want to come home early and keep me company that's good too." She kissed him again. "Let me check on her."

She walked down the hall and toward the room in the back. When she opened the door Carlita was in bed staring at the television. "How you doing?" Spy asked.

She nodded. "Fine." She sighed. "I guess."

Spy walked deeper into the room and sat on the edge of the bed. Carlita, who was paralyzed from the neck down, could only talk. She couldn't move, walk or do anything for herself. In the beginning she begged Spy and Poe to kill her, to put her out of her misery, but neither would comply.

Instead they moved her with them to L.A., in the hopes of giving her a better life. Although they found comfort in each other the opposite was true for her. At night, while they laid in each other's arms, she was alone with the memories that had she not plotted to get revenge against Mo, none of this would've happened. The memories made her dark and bitter and she didn't want to live that way. But with them refusing to kill her she had no choice.

She was too helpless to take her own life.

"Do you want anything?" Spy asked.

"Just to be left alone."

She stood up and walked toward the door. Before leaving she turned around and said, "I love you, cousin." Spy sighed. "Very much."

"I know," she responded, trying to hide the hate she had brewing in her heart. "Please leave me alone. For a little while."

Later when Carlita's nurse came to wash her up she remembered having a thought right before her life changed. Right before she was shot. She felt she didn't need anything or anybody. And with her being paralyzed not only did she realize it wasn't the case, she would have to live with it for the rest of her life.

CARTEL PUBLICATIONS
PRESENTS
NEFARIOUS
T. STYLES
NATIONAL BEST SELLING AUTHOR OF RAUNCHY

The Cartel Publications Order Form
www.thecartelpublications.com
Inmates **ONLY** receive novels for $10.00 per book.
(Mail Order **MUST** come from inmate directly to receive discount)

Shyt List 1	________	$15.00
Shyt List 2	________	$15.00
Shyt List 3	________	$15.00
Shyt List 4	________	$15.00
Shyt List 5	________	$15.00
Pitbulls In A Skirt	________	$15.00
Pitbulls In A Skirt 2	________	$15.00
Pitbulls In A Skirt 3	________	$15.00
Pitbulls In A Skirt 4	________	$15.00
Victoria's Secret	________	$15.00
Poison 1	________	$15.00
Poison 2	________	$15.00
Hell Razor Honeys	________	$15.00
Hell Razor Honeys 2	________	$15.00
A Hustler's Son 2	________	$15.00
Black and Ugly	________	$15.00
Black and Ugly As Ever	________	$15.00
Year Of The Crackmom	________	$15.00
Deadheads	________	$15.00
The Face That Launched A Thousand Bullets	________	$15.00
The Unusual Suspects	________	$15.00
Miss Wayne & The Queens of DC	________	$15.00
Paid In Blood (eBook Only)	________	$15.00
Raunchy	________	$15.00
Raunchy 2	________	$15.00
Raunchy 3	________	$15.00
Mad Maxxx	________	$15.00
Quita's Dayscare Center	________	$15.00
Quita's Dayscare Center 2	________	$15.00
Pretty Kings	________	$15.00
Pretty Kings 2	________	$15.00
Pretty Kings 3	________	$15.00
Silence Of The Nine	________	$15.00
Silence Of The Nine 2	________	$15.00
Prison Throne	________	$15.00
Drunk & Hot Girls	________	$15.00
Hersband Material	________	$15.00
The End: How To Write A Bestselling Novel In 30 Days (Non-Fiction Guide)	________	$15.00

Upscale Kittens	________	$15.00
Wake & Bake Boys	________	$15.00
Young & Dumb	________	$15.00
Young & Dumb 2:	________	$15.00
Tranny 911	________	$15.00
Tranny 911: Dixie's Rise	________	$15.00
First Comes Love, Then Comes Murder	________	$15.00
Luxury Tax	________	$15.00
The Lying King	________	$15.00
Crazy Kind Of Love	________	$15.00
And They Call Me God	________	$15.00
The Ungrateful Bastards	________	$15.00
Lipstick Dom	________	$15.00
A School of Dolls	________	$15.00
KALI: Raunchy Relived	________	$15.00
Skeezers	________	$15.00

Please add $4.00 **PER BOOK** for shipping and handling.

The Cartel Publications * P.O. BOX 486 OWINGS MILLS MD 21117

Name: ________

Address: ________

City/State: ________

Contact# & Email: ________

Please allow 5-7 BUSINESS days before shipping.

The Cartel Publications is NOT responsible for prison orders rejected.

NO PERSONAL CHECKS ACCEPTED

STAMPS NO LONGER ACCEPTED